YOUR BLOOD AND BONES

Also by J. Patricia Anderson

CHILDREN OF THE TREES
Daughters of Tith

J. Patricia Anderson

YOUR BLOOD AND BONES

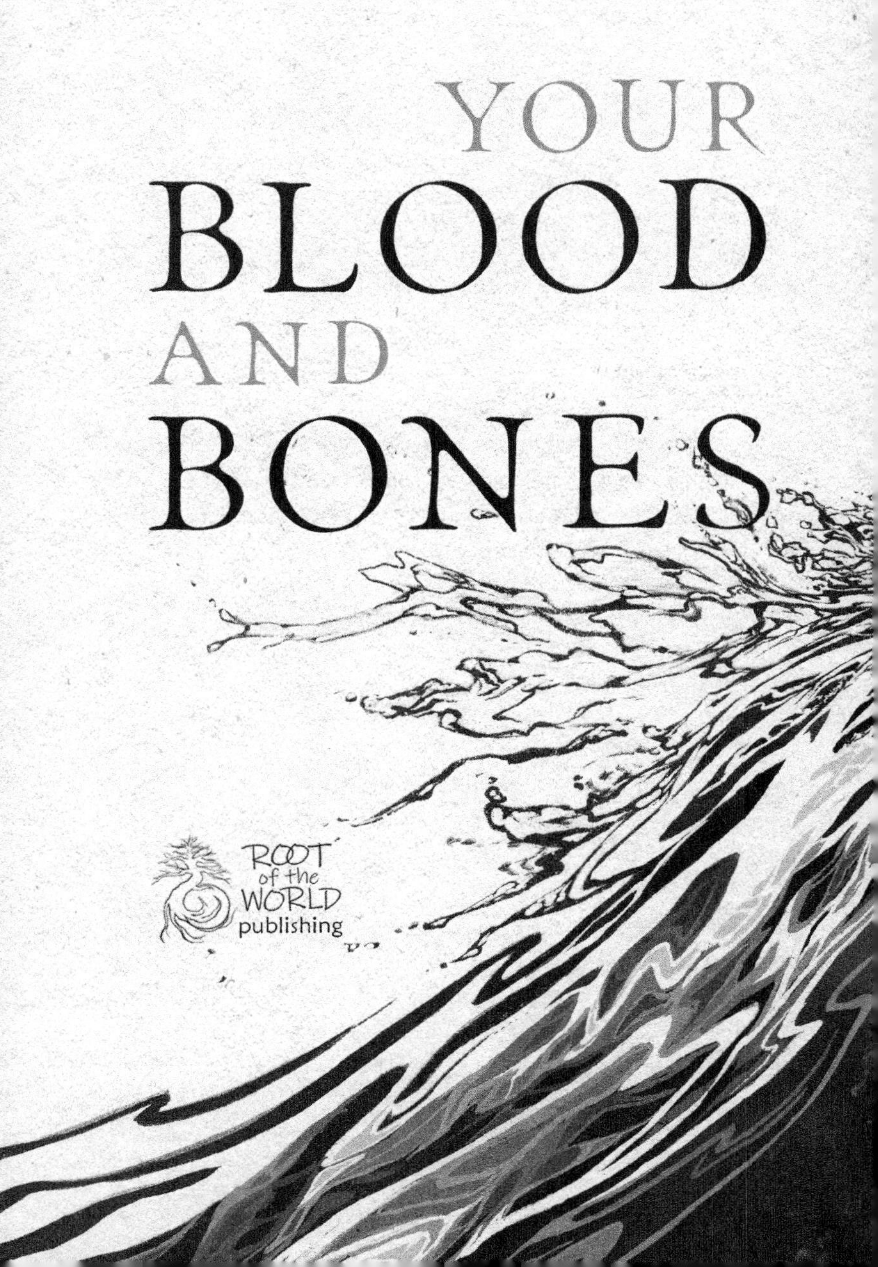

YOUR BLOOD AND BONES

Paperback, 1st edition
Published by Root of the World Publishing on August 27th, 2023

The story, all names, characters, and incidents portrayed in this production are fictitious. No identification with actual persons (living or deceased), places, buildings, and products is intended or should be inferred.

Cover and interior title page illustration by Jenna Vincent
Cover design by VM Designs

ISBNs: 978-1-7782881-4-2 (ebook), 978-1-7782881-5-9 (paperback), 978-1-7782881-6-6 (hardcover)

Root of the World Publishing
rootoftheworldpublishing.com

For Raggi

Content warnings

YOUR BLOOD AND BONES includes body horror, self-harm, and gore.

YOUR BLOOD AND BONES

THE SLUSHY SNOW BURNED the girl's bare feet. The rough volcanic rocks beneath the thin moss cut them. She closed her eyes against the sting and tripped. Icy pain bloomed on her palms as she sought to catch herself. She managed to protect her face but jarred her shoulder on something solid. She didn't get up.

The boy crashed on ahead through the darkness and she thought he would leave her. He cursed, and stopped.

"Get up," he called. "We have to keep moving."

The girl curled into a ball and lay on her side, bitter cold soaking her nightgown. The numbing wet and the radiating pain in her hands and feet distracted from the deep ache in her joints. "No."

"Please."

Exhaustion sought to claim her. She was bone weary from hiding for so long only to be found out in the middle of the damp spring night. The urge to give up—to simply stop and be done—warred with the bite of the ice against her.

"I didn't save you so you could quit on me—"

"You haven't saved me from anything," she said. "I'm still going to die."

She had been warm and secure in her bed an hour ago. In a home that had always felt safe, until she realised what she was. Her family was wealthy, settled in the community. Her parents and brothers had loved her. Something she would never have doubted before this night.

She had been far better off than most in the village until the transformation began. She should have had an easy life. Should have been allowed to grow up. To live long. But not anymore. That hadn't been guaranteed to her for years.

The darkness was quiet for a moment. Then she felt the boy's hands on her arms. He lifted her easily, strong from work on the farm. His grip withdrew and she remained on her feet.

"You have to do this much yourself. I can't carry you and still get away."

His breath frosted the air and his black hair reflected the weak moonlight. Steam rose from his shoulders. The girl looked at the ground. Maybe he could see her face in this light. She couldn't see his.

"We can slow down," he said. "But we can't stop. They'll be busy enough with that fire not to have left yet but when they do they'll move fast."

He turned away—all his words spoken—and in the end she followed.

His form ahead of her was a void of deeper blackness in the night. She was dressed for bed—almost naked in the melting snow. He was better dressed—strangely overdressed for bed, in a long-sleeved shirt and pants—but probably still freezing, the fabric thin and worn. He wore boots, while her feet were bare. She wished he had put on a coat.

What had he been thinking, saving her? They wouldn't survive the night like this. She would die regardless, had been about to die—she flinched away from the memories—but he'd chosen to doom himself with her. Even without the cold he was marked for having helped her. For saving her from the fate that befell all like her. Did he understand what he had done?

Behind them, the night grew bright. The girl saw the boy's face clearly in the red glow when he turned back to the village. She did the same, looking back at their home. At what was once their home but never would be again. The fire had spread to the brush around the houses. The sight disturbed her. How could it burn the damp spring bushes? It shouldn't even have burned the houses—slick with melting snow and ice. An evil fire. The girl understood why the villagers had been so afraid when the boy set it.

He turned away from the light and continued across the heath. The girl followed. Her hands and feet were fully numb now, rendering her clumsy but strangely comfortable. When the boy stopped she stood on the frozen soil without flinching.

He waded into a stand of gnarled birch, just visible in the pale silver light—tangled limbs growing close to the thawing ground to ward against the whipping wind—and ducked under their branches, still naked since the winter.

"What's this?" the girl asked, words slurred and quieter than she had meant them to be. The skin on her face felt stiff, her lips as clumsy as her feet.

Dead leaves rustled as the boy pulled aside a mess of twisted branches to reveal a trench dug in the ground. Shadowed shapes covered in the folds of fabric filled it.

"I gathered everything I could through the winter. I have enough for you, though I doubt any of it will fit. I didn't expect to leave like this so we're going to have to wear as much as we can. You can help me carry the rest."

A shiver ran through the girl, and she was afraid because she should have shivered more. If she was cold enough to stop shivering she was in trouble. The boy handed her a long-sleeved man's shirt and a threadbare coat. She took them with fumbling fingers. She turned away from him to put them on, edging her frosted nightgown down her body. It would be wet when it thawed, and the clothes were dry. She avoided looking at her own exposed skin.

A vivid memory of her mother grabbing her arm intruded in the dark, flashing across the blackness before her. The look on her mother's face at the sight of the girl's skin... She closed her eyes tight and awkwardly pulled the shirt on, little dexterity left in her hands. She held them against the back of her neck to warm for a moment then squeezed them under her arms.

The boy made an impatient sound and she went back to the clothes, covering herself with the coat, trying to seal in any remaining heat. When she turned back to him he had piled more at her feet. Why did he have this? She put the rest of the clothing on as if in a dream. She barely registered the touch of the cloth against her skin, feeling only the core of her limbs now, her senses retreating to where it was warmer.

Everything the boy gave her was much too big, but with some adjustments she could stop it from falling off. She was grateful for the coverage, finally able to hide her problematic skin. The boy dressed similarly, in bulky layers, but the clothing actually fit him. He handed her a second, newer coat and a heavy bag to strap on her back.

"Less for me to carry alone, at least."

"Why do you have this ready?" the girl asked. "Like you were going to flee the village into the night."

"I wouldn't have fled into the night." He ducked out of the birch copse, leaving the empty cache revealed, and walked past her. "If things had gone as planned I would have left in broad daylight, without anyone chasing me."

She began to shiver violently as the clothing held the remaining heat in her body against her. Heat that would keep her alive. Until the villagers caught them.

"Don't you know what I am?" she shouted at his back.

He had to know. There could be no other reason to have to save a girl from her deranged family, in a frenzy of madness, about to cut her to pieces and burn the remains. If he hadn't known before he would know now. He must have seen her skin.

The boy looked back, and suddenly the night just beyond him was full of red light. It reflected on his face. Fire. The air reverberated with the first slow beat of a drum.

"They're coming now," he said. "You're going to have to run with me."

They ran. The heavy bag knocked against the girl's back and the overly large boots thudded on the rocks and threatened to trip her. She hadn't run in a year, at least. Not since she'd grown too afraid of any injury that might expose her. The exertion was unexpected and extreme. Her breath burned her frozen lungs and the inside of her throat.

The boy ran towards the sea. The girl struggled to follow. The slush of spring slid under her feet. Sucking mud slowed her steps. It almost took the boots. The boy staggered ahead of her as the land trended downwards, but kept his footing.

Why run to the water? There was no boat on the island that would be unattended. There was no wood to make their own. And they wouldn't have time. The sound of the drum rose behind them. There would be no escape.

Then the girl remembered the boy's father might have access to a boat. They were farmers, his family, and dirt poor as far as she knew. Before the boy's mother had died she had sometimes done the washing for the girl's mother, for extra food, maybe with a penny on the side. But his father went on supply trips to the mainland for the village. No one from the island would travel the sea in winter but the season changed. It was almost time. There could be a boat on the beach.

The boy fell when they got to the bottom of the rocky, mossy slope, his speed propelling him onto his hands and knees against the earth. The girl slid down the last bit of the slope and sat beside him, exhausted, on the broken ice.

"Come on," he said, getting to his feet. "We can't stop now."

The girl was about to protest when she realised there was no point in arguing. Either they would die running or they'd die sitting. It wasn't really up to the boy where she died. She didn't have to get up. He wouldn't wait for her. He wouldn't choose to die sitting, or he wouldn't have rescued her in the first place. She met his eyes in the dim light. There was no reason for her to run except that he had saved her. He had chosen to save her and really, to die with her. Maybe she owed him a fight.

And maybe there was a boat.

She stood. The boy ran towards the shore, scuffing the untouched black silt of the field before the beach. The girl looked back across the heath and saw points of light in the night. Torches. Her heart felt like it was going to explode.

Ahead, the boy dropped out of sight behind the great bulwark of moss and grass that marked the beginning of the beach proper, where the high tide waves carved out the lower beach and the seabirds nested. The girl caught up and started to lower herself down as competently as she could, but when the wind from the sea hit her face she was rocked by the stench of death.

The moon broke through the clouds and the boy was revealed clearly below. He stood on a carpet of dead creatures. Feathers and bones and matted fur, clotted blood and white or rotted-away eyes. There were no seabirds nesting in the tunnels under the overhang edge, only more bodies, spilling out of the earth like a waterfall of gore. Snapped necks. Broken limbs and wings.

"What is this?" The girl backed away from the overhang towards the villagers' torches, gaining on them across the field.

"No time," the boy said, reaching up the slope to take her hand. "They've almost got us."

She let him pull her down into the mass of dead animals, cringing as the thawing carcases squelched under her too-large boots. Her head swung wildly towards the sea. The waves rolled in under the bright moonlight and there was no break in them. Nothing on the black beach. No boat. The tiny bones of the creatures cracked as she shifted her weight. At head height someone looked back at her with dead white eyes. Human eyes. She screamed. The boy pulled her against his chest and she let him.

There was nowhere to go if there was no boat. Why had the boy brought her to this place? Who was the man who hung out of the seabird houses like a scarecrow missing its stuffing?

She looked over the boy's shoulder and this time she studied the dead man, lit up in the silvery light of the moon. "That's the blacksmith."

Their blacksmith had been missing from the village for a month. Ran away to the mainland in the middle of winter, someone said, but they all knew it was just as likely he had been wandering drunk on the heath and gotten lost in one of the heavy snows. They'd searched for a few days before abruptly stopping. After that everyone knew he was out of reach or dead. The girl's father had planned to send for a new one come spring. He would do that soon. The previous blacksmith's body must have been preserved by the cold. All of this must have been.

"I'm going to set a fire." The boy held her in front of him with both hands on her shoulders. He looked into her eyes. "You hear the drum. You see the torches. You know they're coming. They will kill us."

"What happened to the blacksmith?" she asked. "Why is his body here?"

He let her go and she slumped down amongst the corpses. The drum beat a steady thumping, nearer and nearer. Smoke curled before the girl's eyes and she turned to see the boy with a handful of hay, gently burning. He placed it on the ground between the remains and rolled up his sleeves. Her eyes widened.

The fitful light of the small fire illuminated him, and there, in his snow-pale skin, were the shadows of grey feathers. A ridge ran up each of his arms from his wrists, jutting bone almost breaking the skin. She smoothed a hand over her own wrist, just starting to show the same pattern. Now she knew why he had saved her.

But that meant he was a monster. Just like she was. And she knew what must have happened to the blacksmith.

The boy pressed hard on the growing ridge of bone and the skin that concealed it split. Blood spilled out, hard to see in the dim light but the girl knew it would be darker than it should be, almost purple. It gushed into the growing fire and black smoke billowed around them. The boy pushed the severed skin aside and dug into his flesh. The girl watched in horror. She had done the same before, but it was worse to see it done to someone else.

The boy must have done it before too. He barely flinched. The girl turned away to be sick and found herself staring into the rotted eyes of a rabbit. Smoke swirled against her cheek and stung her throat. Reality shifted. The rabbit moved.

The choking smoke filled the lee of the bulwark. The boy breathed it in deeply and coughed. The girl covered her nose and mouth with her sleeve but the smoke was impossible to escape. She remembered the unstoppable fire the boy had set in the village. She stood straight and looked back over the ridge towards their burning home and the mountain behind it. Their people were coming. Close enough to be seen clearly now, despite the dark.

Bodies shifted under her feet. The dead things began to move and as they did they screamed. The boy breathed loudly. He coughed and laughed. The girl felt him there, not just the warmth of his body near hers, but the haze of his mind. And the minds of the animals. And of the blacksmith. Frenetic, nonsensical thoughts assaulted her. The decomposing thoughts of the dead.

The boy dug something out of his arm, long and flexible, his blood still dripping into the smoking fire. It was a feather, the barbs weighed down with gore. He dropped it into the small flame and the smoke grew to cover them.

The village people charging towards them slowed. The silver moonlight grew grey. The dead animals under the girl writhed away, dragging their broken bodies haltingly across the black sand, towards the sea. The boy called after them, urging them on, commanding them to enter the water. The film of their minds stayed with the girl, clung to her. The blacksmith's decaying body arched its back and dragged itself after them.

The boy knelt in the space as they left. He smothered the small flames and scraped the white ash into his hands, gathering it into a wax paper bag and putting it in the pack he carried. Then he stood and moved to follow his dead subjects.

The girl's eyes wouldn't focus. She tried to watch the boy but flares of false light distracted her. Her focus was drawn to the island instead. The black sand the boy walked onto was made of crushed bones and dead fish and the rock of the island. The rock of the island was suffused with the remains of those who had lived there and those who had visited, never to leave. The girl felt them all.

She looked back over the ridge at the advancing mob. Behind them, past the heath, past the village, the mountain reared up. The smoke in the girl's lungs let her feel the fire deep beneath the earth. Molten rock. Molten death. Death was in the earth and in the sky and in the sea. The mountain was lit with it. Unearthly voices spoke to the girl as her vision faded, tunnelled, and locked onto the summit. The fire could burst from the mountain and come down to sweep the villagers away. Join their bodies to the bodies of their predecessors. The fire only needed to be freed and it could remove their rotten false love from the earth. Just because someone was becoming a monster, did that mean you could forget they were also a person? Your neighbour? Your sister?

Your daughter?

The girl's mind filled with images of her family's faces as they attacked her. Mother rushing into her room in the night, wrenching the sheets away to reveal her changing flesh. Grabbing the girl's arm as she roused from sleep and pulling her near to reveal the shadows under her skin.

Mother's face contracting into a rictus of hate and fear. Screaming to bring the girl's brothers bursting through the door behind her. Father, standing back, more disappointed than anything. Did the girl see a tear in his eye or had she imagined it? He didn't stop them, and quickly she was in the square, thrown on the ground in front of the others. Then the boy had come. He was big for his age—a full adult really, at eighteen—but he shouldn't have been able to fight them. Not all of them at once. But they had been afraid. First of the boy, then of the fire.

The boy called to her and she was freed of the memory. She turned away from the mountain. The dead things had made it to the water. They grasped at each other as they entered the surf, forming a seething, floating carpet of living death. She ran towards them. Towards the boy.

The world seemed to slow again as their eyes met. Without words she showed him the mountain and its promise of revenge. The molten fire that was available to them with the power they shared. Power over the dead. Power over life and death, which were one and the same. Both looked upon the approaching villagers and thought for a frozen moment. In the end they left the fire where it was.

The girl stepped into the water and took the boy's offered hand, climbing onto the writhing mass of bodies.

They were drawn away from the shore by the dead's grasping feet, their paddling beneath the surface. There was a wolf's head by the girl's thigh, partially submerged, half its face rotted off and the desiccated fur floating around its bones. It gargled in the water, one broken foreleg rising and falling, trying to push the boat out, out into the blue. Away.

Cold water crashed over the girl from behind as they entered the waves. The villagers arrived on the shore and milled there, visible in the moonlight and by the light of the torches they carried. Shouting. Drumming. A flaming arrow flew past the girl's head, seeming to slow as it slipped by. She watched the current it made in the dark air. But she wasn't afraid.

The boy lay flat on his back on the boat made of bodies, unmoving when cold water splashed him. As the smoke left her lungs the girl became more aware of what she was kneeling on. She opened her mouth to speak but found she couldn't. Instead she joined the boy and watched the blacker shadow of the island disappear in the darkness until the rhythmic motion of the waves lulled her to sleep.

THE GIRL STARTLED AWAKE. The half-bald skull of a stag met her when she opened her eyes and she had to stifle a scream. Not that it would have mattered. She could scream now and no one would hear her. She almost did, just because she finally could.

The boy sat across from her on the raft of corpses, his face tilted up to look into the night sky, the bright moonlight illuminating his profile. Nothing monstrous about his face. At least not yet. But what he had done to the blacksmith and the animals was monstrous. Could she see it in his eyes? He turned to her and the light left his face.

"You're awake," he said.

The girl sat up on the raft, trying not to think of the things that supported her and the things she pressed against as she shifted. The blacksmith could be one of them, his dead eyes staring up at the sky or maybe into the depths of the sea. The girl's hand brushed soft fur and the familiar sensation was comforting before she realised the perversion of it.

Darkness and the sounds of water surrounded them. She was not afraid of the sea. Growing up on an island had given her a respect for the danger it held but had also made her comfortable with it. With the darkness of it at night and the rage of it during storms.

She looked up at the stars. They formed a shape like the eye of some fierce creature the north had never seen. It winked back at her, no clouds to block its sight. Clearer weather than the girl was used to on the island. She was grateful for it. A spring storm could sink them.

"What happened back there?" she asked. "How did we do that?"

The dead animals didn't seem to move much anymore, and she couldn't feel their minds. She almost didn't believe what had happened. It felt like a dream. Or a nightmare. But the dead animals *had* moved to the water and tangled themselves into a raft. The girl and the boy had escaped, and they sat on that raft of rot now.

"You know the stories," the boy answered, easing himself down against the fur and desiccated flesh.

"The stories say we're supposed to be dead. If we survive the sea, the first person who sees us and knows what we are will try to kill us and even if they fail, and the next does, and the next, we will still die."

"Is that all you know?" The boy turned his eyes towards the stars, revealing his strong brow and straight nose.

She didn't know a lot. The facts were closely guarded. Illegal. Forbidden. The girl had a small library in her home—more books than anyone else in the village—many more than the boy could possibly have ever seen since his family had almost nothing. All those books and still, she had never seen one on the subject. She only knew the stories told by children in the dark.

"That's the only thing that matters," she said stubbornly. "There is nothing else to know."

"How can you say that after what happened?"

The girl sniffed and turned away. It only made sense for him to know as little as she did. But the raft...

"As if you know any more," she said to cover her growing unease.

"I do, actually. We had books about it."

"If such a book exists it must be forbidden. How did *you* get something like that?"

He shrugged in the moonlight.

"My mother had them." There was something in his voice. A catch. "Secret books. Old. Handwritten. About the Black Mages and monsters and their magic. I think she knew about me. Before she died."

"Or she was a witch," the girl responded.

"Maybe she was."

The girl rolled her shoulders under the weight of the bag she had forgotten remained tightly strapped to her. The bag the boy had carried sat to the side of him.

"I hope you packed food," the girl said. "And water."

"Of course." The boy leaned over and undid the strings that held the top of his bag closed. "We'll eat when we make landfall. But for now I want to show you something."

He rummaged through its contents and removed two packets wrapped tightly in oiled paper and a third in soft cloth. He unwrapped them and revealed the wax paper bag of ash, a flint and steel, and a mortar and pestle. He placed each of them gently to the side. The girl tried not to think about what they rested on. Her vision shifted, still affected, and she saw one of the animals snap the flint and steel down its holey gullet. She blinked and the tools remained there in the silver light. She shuddered.

"That's the ash from the fire you set," she said. The boy nodded. "Flint and steel for campfires. What are the mortar and pestle for?"

"Not just campfires," the boy replied, ignoring her question. "The books I read talked about the magic we can do if we're willing. The magic the Black Mages were looking for when they set the villagers on our kind."

"So the boat was planned?"

He shrugged. "No wood for a boat."

The girl sighed. She had to adjust to being the less educated in this situation. Everything about the boy, everything about their history in the village told her he should know nothing. Nothing of import. Possibly more about survival than she knew, but still, not necessarily. This was one subject she barely knew anything about, yet he indicated he did. She would have to accept his words.

"*Kill the monsters when they're found.*" The familiar refrain came easily to her. Drilled into her head as a child and obsessively, compulsively repeated over and over since she found the first feather under her skin. "*No matter who they used to be. Drain their blood. Butcher their flesh. Grind their bones to dust.*"

"*Wrap it all and sink it in the sea,*" the boy continued. "*Leave nothing, lest some weak soul be tempted by the dark power bestowed upon those desperate enough to break the covenant. Desperate enough to use the remains.*"

"That's all I know," she said.

"Once the Black Mages realised they couldn't get to all the villages with emerging monsters they didn't want anyone challenging their power. They taught the villages to dispose of their own monsters. That's us," he said. "But no one ever considers that the monsters themselves might be desperate enough to break the covenant. To use the remains."

Not remains, in this case. The blood and flesh and bones of the living. Their blood and flesh and bones. That was what the boy had done with the fire. Used his own blood and the feathers that grew in his body for access to dark magic.

The boy returned the items to their wrapping and put them back in the bag, tightening the closure until it was secure.

How secure against water, the girl didn't know. She frowned.

"You were stupid to get caught so easily," he said.

She was reminded of all his preparations, the reason for which had been made clear when he revealed his skin to her on the beach. Preparations that must have taken months, if done secretly. She hadn't made any. As soon as she knew she'd figured she was dead.

"You were stupid to save me," she responded.

"It was that or do this alone." He lay back on the blanket of corpses, rippling gently on the waves. "I'm tired now. You must be too. We should rest."

She watched him as his breathing became shallow and rhythmic. Do what alone? Die alone? She still didn't understand the escape. She cringed at the thought of her family's faces again, in the firelight. Almost more horrifying than the faces of the dead things that made up her bed as she lay down beside the boy and succumbed to sleep.

THE GIRL WOKE TO a growing lightness in the sky. The sea remained gentle and a thin layer of clouds screened them from the harsh gaze of the morning sun. She was still cold, but the shredded fur surrounding her had kept what heat she had close. The ache in her bones made itself known as she sat up on the unsteady surface.

She found the boy staring at a dark wall of clouds in the distance. A storm on the water. He had taken off his coat despite the crisp sea wind, maybe in an attempt to let it dry. The unnatural bone spurs that protruded along his shoulder blades and spine were stark against the thin shirt he wore.

"What's the plan?" The girl turned in a circle and could clearly see the mainland now, seeming to stretch on forever to one side of the raft. The mountain on their island broke up the flat horizon to the other. Maybe the boy had been so focused on escape he didn't care where they went as long as it was away. "Where are we going?"

"We're going to the mainland. The current in this channel will take us to the great beach eventually."

"Why? The people there will know us just as well as those on the island did."

"We're going to be cured."

So that explained his purpose in escaping. The girl had never heard of a cure, but that wasn't surprising. The monsters were said to be killed immediately upon being found out. Or at least that was what the children said. What the stories said. They weren't meant to escape. If any had escaped they must have done so as the boy would have done. Quietly. Secretly. Intelligently. Leaving no stories of success to be told.

The girl shook her head at their luck. If it weren't for the island and the lack of boats available to follow them they'd never have made it. An escape wasn't feasible in most cases. Not for young adults that were little more than children. Not for the poor who had nothing. And most of the monsters wouldn't have had hope. Despite her privilege, the girl hadn't planned an escape. She hadn't seen the point.

"How can we be cured of this?" she asked.

"I don't know. I only know where we need to go."

"And where is that?"

"To a Black Mage on the mainland, not far from our island. My father used to do supply runs"—the boy paused and turned to her—"for your father, actually. He's travelled to the mainland more than anyone else I know. One day he told me there was a Black Mage who says she can cure it, just beyond the mainland shore, in a meadow deep inside the great forest. Should be easy to find."

"It's not just a lure?"

The boy frowned. "You'd think so, but my father insisted."

The girl looked at the boy with new eyes. His poor family had proven useful again. Not like hers, who had contributed nothing except an accelerated escape. "He must have known too."

"My father?"

"Like your mother. It sounds like they both knew."

The boy was quiet for a moment. "They didn't help me much if they knew."

"At least they didn't try to kill you, like mine did."

He turned away. "My father needed the help on the farm. The villagers would have figured it out eventually. Like the blacksmith did."

So that explained the dead man. “You were friends, weren’t you?”

The boy’s shoulders slumped. Too friendly, obviously. Friendly enough for the blacksmith to notice the change. Not friendly enough to be safe, it seemed. The girl had thought about telling someone when she first noticed. Although given the boy’s escape plan she doubted he had told the blacksmith. He was just found out. She hadn’t trusted anyone enough to get close, and she’d trusted less and less as she lost friends with her self-imposed distance. She’d almost told her youngest brother once. Maybe if she had it would be him who sat across the width of a raft from her instead of the boy. Or maybe she’d have died years ago, before the boy even knew he was a monster.

She had suffered in silence instead. Alone, but alive. She had always known it was never going to go away. There was no escaping it and it would only get worse, would only end in death. It had felt like it was becoming pointless to hide it, just before her family found out.

The girl looked at the distant storm, not so distant now. “Is that going to come for us?”

The boy followed her gaze. “It may. Looks like a bad one.” He took his bag from the valley in the bodies beside him and strapped it to his back again. The girl looked at hers and considered doing the same. The boy turned to her. "The orcas are a bigger threat at this time of year."

"You're not serious?" The girl raised an eyebrow at him. "We're sitting on a boat made of meat."

"I am. I told you I had a plan to leave. It didn't include fleeing in the night and it didn't include crossing the channel this early in the spring. We'll just have to hope we don't run into any of the pods the fisherpeople sighted last week."

The girl shuddered. She'd only seen orcas once before, when she was very young. A pod was sighted off the coast, tossing seals high into the air before devouring them. Her father had thought she needed to see it. Her stomach had disagreed. She wasn't afraid of the sea but that didn't include the things it contained. The things she didn't have to deal with by staying on dry land.

"It's too late now anyway," he said. "We can't control this raft. Might as well relax until we make landfall."

She frowned but sat back on the bodies and fixated on the approaching mainland. From this distance she could already see the great forest that covered the land beyond the beach. There were few trees on their volcanic island and those they did have were squat and gnarled. The prospect of seeing the big ones before she died was exciting. Seeing them even once.

She had always dreamed of going to the mainland. Everyone on the island did. It was out of reach for most, but not for the girl. She might have gone there to get married, in a different life. There was no one eligible in the village. Maybe she still could, since the boy had talked about a cure. Or maybe she could go home.

"If we can be cured, why burn the village down? Will they let us come back after that?"

"I didn't have much of a choice." The boy gave her a pointed look. "In any case, I'm not going back."

"But it's all we know–"

"Don't you see? We're not truly monsters, but *they* are. They became monsters when they saw an innocent girl in her bed and decided to butcher her in the town square. They were going to kill you. Your family was going to kill you. You can forgive them?"

She felt tears in her eyes as she remembered their changed faces. So hateful. So vicious. So afraid. "No."

"Me neither. And would they ever believe we were actually cured?"

The girl considered that. Probably not. What would a cure even mean? A stop to the transformation? A reversal of their symptoms? It seemed impossible. Too good to be true.

"You're sure we can be cured?" she asked.

"I am. I meant it when I told you we weren't going to die. There is hope."

The sky grew darker suddenly. Waves rocked the corpse raft and wind whipped the decaying fur off the animals. Shreds of it streamed behind them.

"I guess we won't see the orcas," the boy said.

The girl looked up into an approaching wall of water. "The storm."

The waves got higher. The wind grew more intense. The mainland loomed to the south. Safe. Tempting. But the girl knew its closeness was deceptive. She knew the water well enough for that.

Once she and her youngest brother had tried to swim to the island from an old fishing boat that had capsized. They'd stolen it and struck out into the waves only to find it wasn't guarded for a reason. From the sinking frame the shore hadn't looked far at all and she was sure they could make it. They were both strong swimmers. But the island had been much farther away than it looked. She had dropped her shoes and nearly all her clothing as she swam, dragging her brother behind her in the end, and they'd still never have survived if one of the fishermen hadn't been out and seen them slowly drowning just off shore. She and the boy were dressed too heavily now. The boots alone would sink them.

"We can't swim there," she said, as the boy looked ready to abandon the shuddering raft. "We'd never make it."

"I could make it." He looked back at her and seemed to consider if he could save her as well.

"I don't think you could," she said.

"Do you think the raft will survive the storm?"

The raft of corpses was rammed by a rogue wave and the girl was thrown to the side, falling among the fur and bones and digging her fingers into something slimy to hold on. The rain came, whipping across the raft in torrents. They were soaked in moments.

"I don't think it will," she shouted when they were in the next valley between waves. The wet flesh beneath her fingers came apart as they were rocked again.

"We have to swim!" the boy shouted back.

He held the straps of the bag of supplies on his back with all his strength, his thin shirt sodden, his coat forgotten. The girl's bag shifted freely between two thick bones in the middle of the raft. She drew it to her. That should be the first thing she ditched, she knew. But if they could survive the sea they would need clean water. They would need to eat. They definitely needed the flint in the boy's bag.

"No!" she shouted. "We can't! Not with all this weight on us and so far to go."

Terror gripped her, at the raging sea and the dead that supported them. She still wanted to live, it turned out. She had wanted to live for a fleeting moment when her mother pulled her out of bed and her brothers threw her in the street. She had wanted to live, if only to destroy them. There was no one to fight now but the cold and the wind and the water. Still, she found she wanted to live. The joints in her fingers ached with cold and numbness as she pulled herself over to the boy, trying to find purchase against bones quickly being stripped of rotten flesh.

"What magic is there?" she asked when she got to him. "Is there anything we can do?"

The boy's eyes lit up and he fumbled to open his bag with one hand on the rocking raft. "Fire."

"No good in this."

"The ash." He grappled with the bag as the raging sea shook them. He would lose everything if he kept that up.

"Put it back on!" She stopped him with a hand on his arm. "Is there nothing else?"

The boy's eyes searched, his mind working, scouring his memory for something they could use. Another wave hit them and the raft started to come apart. He reached for her, getting a hold of her arm and forcing them back together against the strength of the storm. She screamed at the pain of his grip but the fear of being lost was worse. He probably couldn't hear her over the crashing water. His mouth moved as if he shouted back. They were knocked together and the girl's vision went black and then cleared.

"Blood!" he shouted against her ear. "Blood alone is another!"

She felt a wildness at his words. The bones of the animals had cut her already. The lacerations on her hands and arms were a stinging heat that remained when the rest of her was numb. The boy held her against him, trying to keep them together. She felt his strength tested as the bodies beneath them bowed to the pressure of the savage sea.

"I have to open the bag," he said, barely audible over the raging winds and water.

She shook her head. When the next wave hit them she let go with one hand. The force of the water and her lessened grip caused her to knock against the boy again. She cried out, but she got her hand to her lips, searching for the pain. Her mouth flooded with the tinny taste of blood.

Nothing happened for a moment and she worried. The waves forced her hand against her lips and she bit down. The chaos of the world around her reigned and there was no break in it, no wave of dead minds to take her away. Would it not work if it was her own blood? Her mouth overflowed with the metal taste. Her teeth were elongated from the budding transformation. They were sharp, tearing, monstrous teeth and they did the job they were meant to do.

Then she sensed the other minds. Faintly. Horrifyingly. The animals beneath her screeched like they had on the beach, only the sound was wet and guttural this time, their throats full of salt water. The boy's mind was absent and she looked at him with worry but found him still strongly gripping the raft and the edge of her coat. She tried to speak to the animals with her mind. *Save us.*

They shrieked. They were aware of the ripping waves. Of the cold—colder than death itself because she forced them to feel. The blacksmith was gone, sunk somewhere on the way to this place. The skull closest to the girl opened its mouth and howled. She was mesmerised by its razor sharp teeth. She saw them as her own, attached to her jaw, cutting up the ribbons that remained of her forearm flesh. *Save us.*

The carpet of dead things shivered. The raft exploded with movement as the next wave hit. The animals began to consume each other and the water frothed as they started to sink.

The girl willed them to save her. To save the boy. *Swim*. Swim to shore. *Save us.*

Rotted muscles clenched around her. Flailing, broken legs and wings sliced through the angry water. The boy was gone, out of her reach, as was much of the raft, but there were enough bodies left to make it, and the girl still felt the minds of those around the boy. Or those she hoped were around him. They had to swim to shore. Use their grasping, thrashing limbs. Use the power they had as dead things, the power to not fear the dark beneath the waves because they were already there in their minds.

The blood in her mouth was washed out by seawater. The animals tore at her and time slowed, each agonising puncture and rip foreseen, anticipated, and experienced. She was under water, then above it, held up on wet fur and bone. She breathed. Waves crashed over her and the float of flesh was pushed on. In what direction she didn't know.

COLD WET LAPPED AT the girl's cheek. She coughed. Her throat throbbed. She choked up water and felt heaviness in her lungs. Her head ached and she was mostly numb. When she tried to move, her arms and legs burned as if being pricked by a thousand needles. Her vision lagged behind the movement of her head, as if she had been frozen and was thawing. She felt nauseated and sunk back down into the sand.

The water lapped at her again. She lay on a beach. The sand was a light brown instead of the black that was typical on the island they had come from. Tiny shells spread throughout it. The girl's mind flashed back to the beach on the island and the otherworldly feeling of lost life those shells held. The sand shifted as the water buoyed her weight and her legs sunk a little deeper when it receded.

Ragged lumps disfigured the smooth waterline along the shore beside her. Her eyes rejected focus but once she was able to see clearly she recognised them as the animals that had made up the raft. She struggled to rise.

When she got to her knees, rough hands gripped her and dragged her up the beach. The boy. Her bones were jarred when he tripped over something. A soft "oof", and she looked up to see he had tripped on the intact torso of a caribou. Whatever had been attached to it that let it propel itself there had been lost in the surf.

The boy sat down heavily. Clearly exhausted.

"What did you do?" he asked.

She forced herself to rise to a sitting position, her frozen body resisting. Her voice was raspy and her throat painful. "It's too cold to stay here. We need to dry off and make a fire."

He sat with his arms around his knees. He appeared to have lost most of his outer clothing in the sea and his boots were gone. The change in him was obvious in the midday light. Ridges of bone that didn't belong stood out under his sodden shirt. Grey feathers burst from some of them, leaving the skin around them red and scabbed. Feathers that had yet to erupt showed dark against his fair complexion from the inside. His nails were long, like the beginnings of claws. Becoming a monster, but still human enough to be beautiful. The girls' cheeks would have reddened if she had any heat in her. She had never stared at someone so rudely before. The boy dropped his arms when he saw her looking at his hands.

"I found a cave," he said.

She spoke before she could stop herself. "We need one far back from the shore, so high tide doesn't enter it."

"I know that." He gave her an exasperated look. "I'm from the same island you are. It's back in the trees. Can you walk?"

She managed to stand and limp after him. He really was beautiful, she realised, as she watched him walk in the daylight. If it weren't for the monster he was becoming she would be tempted by his broad shoulders and lean muscle. If it weren't for the monster *she* was becoming.

The farming must have done it to him. The girl had never looked at him before because he wasn't an option, on the island. Not a serious option, at least, and she wasn't the type to play. Especially after she began to change. She forced herself to look away from him. To focus on surviving.

She still had her boots, was still wearing the two coats and the pants the boy had given her when they made it to his cache during their escape. Only last night. It was amazing so little time had passed. It was hard to tell the time of day when the sky was still slightly darkened from the passing storm, but if she had to guess she would say it must be past noon.

The bag the boy had given her was still strapped to her. It dripped water steadily down her legs. It was a miracle she had made it to shore. She should have sunk into the waves and drowned in minutes. But she remembered the clenching muscles of the carcases. The claws that had gripped her shoulders, a wing over her face. They had saved her. Probably saved the boy, though he seemed to have shed his clothes in an attempt to stay afloat. She realised she didn't know what was in the pack she carried. Maybe she had saved the wrong one.

"Did you lose the bag?" she asked as she followed him.

"No. We made it here with all that weight. Somehow."

They found more bodies as they progressed up the beach, coming to the end of the long yellow bar of sand before they saw the last one. It was a whole wolf—its obvious cause of death a broken back—that had crawled all the way up to the tree line. They stopped to stare at it. The girl flinched away when she met one of its partially maggot-eaten eyes. The other was just an empty socket.

"It's like they were alive when we got to shore," the boy said. "What did you do on the boat?"

The girl felt numb in her mind as well as her body. Like she couldn't think. Like it was frozen.

"You said blood, so I used the blood on my hands and arms. When there wasn't enough I bit myself."

Saying it reminded her of how badly she had bitten her arm. She pulled up her sleeve, not wanting to see but knowing she needed to in case the cuts had to be cleaned or bandaged. She was so cold she didn't know if it hurt. Amazingly, the wounds were mostly closed, leaving nasty scars that looked like they'd taken months to form. Her wounds had always healed quickly, probably an effect of the transformation, but not this quickly. And this was an injury of another scale. It was hard to believe when she knew she had done so much damage. Her arm felt strange but it was functional. She flexed it, feeling only a slight pulling of the skin.

"The blood wasn't as strong as the smoke," she said. "I couldn't feel your mind. I couldn't feel the world."

He didn't ask anything else. He didn't comment on her experience and he didn't ask what she must have done with the animals in her mind to get them to drag herself and the boy through the waves to the mainland. She didn't explain it either. Mostly because she didn't really know.

The girl looked up at the trees instead. The great, straight trunks towered over them, spreading into a dark canopy of green and shadow. Young leaves, probably newly sprouted in this warmer climate. She let out a small sound of awe. The boy was silent, looking into the forest for the second time. The foliage hid the wide sky they'd grown up with, made the world smaller and closer.

The boy walked ahead, into the shadows. The girl hesitated, but followed quickly when she realised he would disappear into the forest without her if she didn't. They walked for a few minutes, the sameness in the pattern of trunks already confusing to the girl, until they came to a wall of rock. A mountain growing out of the earth.

"More like a crevice," she said when she saw the place the boy had called a cave.

"It's shelter."

The bag lay against the rock and the boy's boots were propped upside down to drain. "I thought you lost the boots."

"I didn't want to walk in them while they were that wet." He looked down at her feet. He was right. She would have blisters. "I don't really"—he paused—"I don't think I feel the cold anymore."

She frowned. When he saw the look on her face he backtracked.

"I don't feel it...the same, I guess. I think I'm still cold. I—"

"I must not feel it as badly either," she said, stopping him. "I've felt numb, but I should be so cold I can't function. I should be cold enough to die, and yet I'm still here."

He nodded like he knew what she meant. They sat down on the floor of the forest, covered slightly above by the crack in the rock he had found. It was probably safer than a cave in the end because they could start a fire and not be worried about inhaling the smoke. The heat would be trapped enough to warm them, and it was unlikely anyone would see.

The girl examined the boy's bare arms again. They would have to cover him soon. It was impossible to imagine someone seeing him like that and not knowing what he was. She hugged her coats closer despite their cloying coldness.

The boy went through his bag, removing the flint and steel first and checking them for moisture. The girl watched him in silence. He placed them on a stone near the centre of the shielded area. Then he lay the bag of ash beside them and the mortar and pestle on the ground below. He spread the food he had packed around that. A lot of it looked wet. The girl didn't care. She was ravenous.

"You must have known for a while," she said to distract herself from the hunger.

"I've known for a few years," he said. "I suspected for some time before that. You?"

"I think I was around fourteen when I found out."

"What then, four years?"

"Close to five."

The boy nodded solemnly, commiserating. "Can you check your bag? I want to know how it fared."

She pulled the bag off her back and undid the strings holding it closed, finding two big skins of water. That explained the weight. She took a small sip from one of them. The water seemed clean although it tasted like leather. "It's good."

He nodded. "You should take off your coat. You can't be warm under all that heavy wet."

She removed the bigger coat and laid it out on a rock. She waited on the second one. No reason to remove it until there was heat from the fire.

"I forgot you had two coats. Good. I lost the best one in the sea."

The girl almost laughed. So something had been lost after all. Not the boots. Not the heavy bags. Just one coat. It was ridiculous they hadn't drowned.

The boy left the crevice and returned with an armful of grass and leaves. The tops of them looked dry enough to catch but the fire would be smokey. He searched through the sheltered area and settled on a flat space in a lee between two rocks. He knelt and piled the aspiring tinder there.

"Can I help?" the girl asked, but she hoped he would say no. She was tired and stiff and sore.

"No need. It won't take long." He left again and came back with an array of small branches. These he stood against each other to form a pyramidal cage, stuffing more grass and leaves into it as he built. The girl picked up the flint and steel and moved closer to watch him, anticipating the heat that would come when he was done.

She handed him the tools and he set them beside the wooden pyramid, leaving once more for extra tinder and larger branches. The girl lay back against a rock, her eyes starting to close involuntarily. She fought to stay awake, afraid the cold would kill her if she succumbed, and not wanting to miss the soggy food the boy had brought. It might be the last thing she ever ate.

The boy appeared above her from nothing and she blinked. Had she slept? Maybe she had dreamed all this. Maybe she was actually dead. The boy sat beside her and he must have struck the flint because a spark burned in her eyes. She shifted positions and came back to herself. The boy struck the flint a second time and the spark caught. It nestled in the grass just below his hands and burned brightly. He blew on it gently. Smoke came up. Like the smoke on the shore of the island. The girl shied away from it.

The fire consumed the leaves and grass, grasping at the small cage of sticks that held it. The boy added more kindling as it reached higher. Always reaching. Up, up, to the sky. Once the fire burned steadily the boy added some bigger sticks from a pile he had made and they settled down to warm up.

The girl removed her smaller coat and was left with the sodden man's shirt and pants. She debated not removing them but knew she couldn't warm up with them on. She pulled the shirt off quickly and held it in front of her to protect some of her modesty. The boy watched her undress and she didn't tell him to stop. She couldn't show herself to anyone else like this. Her skin was filling with the dark shadows of bones and feathers that didn't belong just like his was. Becoming the body of a monster.

"You put one of these feathers in the fire on the shore," she said, indicating a dark shadow on her exposed thigh.

The boy looked at her leg for a moment too long and despite the grim situation she smiled inside. It seemed the shadows didn't make her ugly. At least not to him, who had them too. She looked again at his arms and shoulders. At his neck which appeared mostly human still, as hers did—a good thing because it would have been too hard to hide.

The changes were not unattractive. Not really. Only frightening to others. Terrifying to her, when she thought of how her body was all she had to hold her mind. To hold everything she was. She didn't know when the transformation would stop or what it would do to her. Was her mind itself safe from the changes or would it become the mind of someone—or something—else? They may have survived the village mob but if they became monsters in truth, what was that but another kind of death?

She tried not to think of the place on her shoulder where the offending feathers broke her skin. That was not so attractive. But other than that her body was mostly the same. The hidden feathers, shadows deep inside, even the bones that altered her shape, didn't dampen the effect she might have on others. Only their meaning did. But the boy was a monster too. He looked away from her exposed skin and into her eyes.

"I burned a feather," he said, "and the blood and flesh it brought with it. As far as I know anything from our bodies would produce the same effect. Burn feathers, flesh, bones, blood. Breathe in the smoke. You get a raft of dead things."

"Then you took the ash."

He nodded. "I don't know what that will do. Maybe I can eat it or breathe it in if we find ourselves in trouble again."

"Did you hear my thoughts?" The girl remembered the shape of his mind. The minds of the animals and the dead blacksmith.

"I did. I didn't expect that."

"I couldn't hear you when I tasted my blood on the raft."

"Maybe because we both breathed in the smoke. I didn't touch your blood."

They stared at each other, eyes locked and unblinking. The girl was getting used to being with him. It was easy, even though they hadn't spent much time near each other before. Even easier because she didn't have to lie. Didn't have to hide for the first time in so long. She had thought when he saved her that he might be interested in her. A stupid thing to throw your life away for. Now she knew it was more than that. But it still might also be that.

"What other magic can we do?" she asked.

"I'm not sure of everything. I don't know if anyone knows, except maybe the Black Mages. The book only outlined the use of body parts and blood when consumed, burned, combined to create a liniment—"

"A liniment," she whispered. "For healing?"

"I guess."

The girl looked down at the forearm she had savaged on the raft that was now healed. Scarred, but healed. "So that's what the mortar and pestle are for."

"Exactly."

The boy stared into the fire. His eyes seemed oddly reflective. The girl wondered if hers were the same.

"We should stay here overnight," he said. "Eat what we can. Dry as much as possible. Sleep covered, even if we're wet, so no one knows what they've found if they stumble upon us."

"I'm starving," the girl said.

The boy looked over the food he had spread out from the bag. "It's nothing fancy and a lot of it looks unappetising now, but it's all I have."

The girl had to stop herself from reaching out too eagerly when he offered some to her. They ate in silence. The girl savoured the soggy salted meat and crumbled biscuits even though they were far worse than anything she had eaten in her life. Maybe it was because she was so hungry or maybe it was because she hadn't expected to eat again.

Afterwards the boy packed what could be salvaged together and set it beside his drying bag.

"Do you know where we have to go?" The girl's voice sounded better after eating and drinking. The heaviness in her chest from the water she inhaled felt less now. Warmth began in her stomach and met the touch of the fire's heat on her skin.

The boy turned back in the direction of the beach. "I'll look for the island on the horizon in the morning. That should help me orient myself. Then it's south, into the forest to find the meadow."

The girl looked up at all the tall trees again and found them intimidating. "Maybe we can find a road. Or a path."

"Maybe. I don't know what's here exactly." He looked back at her and smiled, showing his monstrous teeth. "Think of it as an adventure. Bet you always wanted to see the mainland."

She smiled faintly back at him. Maybe they wouldn't die. Not yet anyway.

Not yet.

THE GIRL WAS UP before the boy, waking too early because of the cold. She opened her eyes to weak daylight from a nightmare in which she was cast into the village square and set upon by the rabid people. Only this time there was no boy to save her.

Thrown on the cold concrete and stripped. Cut with kitchen knives and burned by household torches, lit hastily in the night. Everyday tools turned to a gruesome task. They killed her slowly. Tied her, hung her upside-down, sliced her open and let her bleed. The nightmare didn't end when she was dead. They dissected her body, separating her flesh and her bones and whatever blood remained. Setting it all ablaze on the black beach, the toxic smoke floating away from the village, and then throwing what was left to the sea. To the orcas or sharks or seabirds.

It wasn't a new nightmare. It wasn't even surprising. It had been the expected end to her life since she found out what she was.

She opened her eyes wide to dispel the images. She had never actually seen it done, this ritual monster murder. The nightmare was her own creation, built from stories told to frighten younger siblings when they already couldn't sleep. The village hadn't had any monsters while she'd been alive. It made sense now, given that she was the one they would have burned.

She shivered against the boy, the fire dead beside them. She had shivered the night before, unable to sleep because of the uncontrollable shuddering—the fire had made her warm enough for the cold to hurt—but the nightmare meant she must have slept eventually. The boy slept soundly against her still, barely moving at all. Barely breathing. She nudged him and he shifted slightly. Still alive.

She lay against him until he woke. He was warmer than she was, and bigger. She pressed against him hesitantly, wondering if he might hold her, but she stopped when one of the bones breaking through at her shoulder blade grazed him. It made her shiver for a different reason. The boy woke shortly afterwards and they stayed by the renewed fire for an hour or so to warm before they set out.

Now the girl trudged through the underbrush behind the boy. Her clothes and boots were still damp but at least they weren't sodden. There was life and warmth in her, as well as a little of the remaining food and clear water.

Trunks and branches swayed gently above. Traversing the forest was unlike anything the girl had encountered growing up on the island. Their village lay in the shadow of the mountain but everything else was laid bare before it. The heath was flat until it met the flat beach which led out to the flat ocean. Above all of that was simply sky. You could get lost in bad weather but when the sky was clear you could see everything. Here there was no vast sky, only tiny moments of it, peeking through the crowns of the trees.

Some of the forest was open, flat, and easy to navigate. The rest was like walking through a tangle of grasping fingers that clawed at the girl's too-big clothes. The boy tried to avoid those places, walking in a zigzag, always angling back to the direction they'd chosen.

They'd selected it based on the morning sun. Finding it rising in the east they were able to pinpoint the island mountain on the horizon. Using the island as reference they were able to confirm the direction they had to walk based on what the boy's father had told him. The girl thought it seemed too easy. Why would the cure be so close to their home? And if it was real, why hadn't she heard about it before?

But at the same time, their village hadn't had any monsters in her lifetime, or in the lifetimes of her parents, until the girl and the boy themselves. She wasn't sure about the elders, but she didn't remember being told personal stories about them at any point in her life. The stories were always mythic. Distanced. They had been terrifying to a child, but unreal in a way. Until they became real for the girl. Until they became real to the village again. Tales of a cure could have died with the last generation to actually see a monster. She looked through the trees towards the boy ahead. As for the convenience of the Black Mage's location, she'd judge that if they made it there.

The pain in the boy's body was obvious from how he walked now. The new bones were sometimes jagged and pressed on their flesh inside. Cutting it. Some of the darkness showing through their skin wasn't feathers. Some of it was bruising. Continually blooming in vivid colour before healing nearly as quickly. The girl's joints ached. Her shoulders and hips and knees. Her fingers. Her neck when she turned it. Something seemed to be growing at the top of her spine.

She looked at her wrist as the long coat shifted and revealed some of her skin. The change seemed to be accelerating. She hadn't been as bad as the boy when they ran away and now she looked like he had when they'd made it to the mainland shore. She hadn't expected that and it terrified her. Then again, she didn't know how long the transformation was meant to take in the first place.

"How did you know?" the boy asked, from up ahead. "What did you notice first, when the change started to come upon you?"

She struggled to catch up to him so he would hear her response. He moved quickly. Maybe he felt the change advancing as well. She considered lying, continuing to hide herself, but why not tell the truth? They would either die or be cured soon, and then it wouldn't matter.

"I thought I was going to bleed for the first time." The words entered the quiet, empty forest and they felt freeing. She had never been able to tell anyone this. The boy stopped and she saw the blush spread on his face. She frowned but continued. "I complained of feeling hot and sick and foggy-headed. Then my stomach hurt and my joints and bones and just everything. My mother made fun of me but I knew she was proud. *'You're becoming a woman,'* she said. But nothing came of it. Then I found the first dark feather in my arm. And I've actually never bled. I fake it."

"All my joints ached too," the boy said. "And it felt like bruising all over my body. I thought it was from the farm work or the beatings... Then I caught a fever. It lasted for two days. A very bad one. They thought I was going to die."

"Good thing they didn't find any of the changes on you then."

"Maybe they did."

The girl walked past the boy, pushing her way through the branches. Nothing ahead of her, just the seemingly unending forest. She breathed in the clean air, the smell of the trees. She was alive, for now, despite the pain. And she could say anything. There was no more need to keep secrets.

"Did you take the feathers out?" the boy asked from behind her.

"I did. The first...I don't know, very many of them."

"I did too." The boy sounded excited now. Voicing things he hadn't been able to tell anyone. The girl understood. She craved his words, craved to share her stories.

"They disgusted me," the girl said, "for a long time. Now I just wish they didn't hurt so much."

The boy's lingering gaze told her that at least he wasn't disgusted by the look of her.

"They really do hurt," he said. "The worst one was...I had a bone shard in my leg. In my calf. I woke in the field one morning—I had been out minding the sheep. I woke, and I couldn't walk. Something inside my muscle was cutting, tearing. I couldn't move or it bit into me. I searched my skin and under the hair there was a kind of scab."

The boy's face was contemplative as he spoke, his eyes unseeing, as if he recited a dream from deep inside, rather than a true memory.

"I ran my fingers over it and I felt the raised edge. I lifted it slightly and found something hard underneath. It hurt, but it was a different kind of hurt."

The girl knew what he meant. Compulsive. Cathartic. "Like picking your teeth with a sliver of wood."

"Yes." He looked at her and met her eyes. "Yes. Much more painful, but that same idea. I lifted the raised edge and found this hard thing. I thought maybe it was a large splinter. Maybe wood. Maybe it got lodged in there when I was working in the stables. I started to dig it out with my fingers and it was big, and it was clearly the thing that stopped me from walking. So I dug it out enough to get a grip, and pulled it from my leg. It was sharp white bone, probably longer and wider than my finger."

The girl knew she should be horrified by the story but she had done the same and worse to herself since her body started growing things that didn't belong. Feathers had poked through her skin and she had pulled them out, bloody and sharp, their edges ripping and slicing as she dragged them from her flesh. Sometimes they broke when they caught on something. Caught on a new shard of bone or cartilage she shouldn't have either. Then she dug those out too.

"How long did that one take to heal?" she asked.

He looked wary, but it was clear he also realised this was a safe place to say anything. They were in it together. They were the same.

"I could walk within the hour."

The injuries the girl incurred trying to rid herself of the offending growths had always healed quickly. But the girl was also sure that anything she removed eventually came back. Or something new grew. Removing things didn't stop the transformation. She had come to know it as inevitable. Discovery was inevitable. Death was inevitable.

"I started gathering the dead animals shortly after that," the boy said. "I found them...interesting. I wanted to look at them, even before I thought to use them. I don't know why. It bothered me at first. I thought maybe my mind was affected by the transformation. That I was a monster in truth."

The girl was surprised. "You didn't kill them?"

"No." He glanced back at her, his eyes seeming to will her to be afraid of him, to run from him. The stories called the children who changed monsters. There was no more reliable information that the girl knew of, except maybe the books the boy had seen. For most people the stories and rumours led to the belief that the so-called monsters were monsters in truth. Violent. Dangerous. It would fit for the boy to kill animals. To have killed the blacksmith. To kill more as he changed. But he said he hadn't. Was an obsession with death something to fear? The girl could run from him. But she wouldn't. She stared right back.

"But you killed the blacksmith."

The boy broke eye contact. He walked a few steps before speaking again, and he didn't answer her. He didn't need to.

"I went far to find the animals," he said instead. "Out on the heath. In the cold. In the beginnings of storms..."

He trailed off and the girl almost left it at that. But she knew what he would have said too well. "You wanted to die."

His eyes flashed back to hers and he walked faster. She kept up.

"I don't want to die," he said. "That's why I'm here."

"The heath in bad weather is death. You wanted to disappear. To die in a way you could control. You didn't want to see them look at you the way they looked at me. You didn't want to be dragged out of your bed by your family. Thrown onto the stones of the square like you were nothing. Like you were—"

"A monster," he said. "You're right. I didn't. Turns out I really hated seeing them do it to you too."

The girl stopped.

The boy turned back to her. "How did you get caught? You look bad now but when we left you barely had a mark on you."

The girl tried not to be affected by his comment. She brushed past him, pulling her sleeves down over her changing wrists and shrugging the coat up to cover her neck better. She wouldn't have answered except that she'd already exposed him. Given voice to his dark, secret thoughts and he hadn't had a choice in that. Once again she was struck with the freedom of impending death. He followed, caught up to her.

"I didn't care anymore," she said. "What's the point? I know we're looking for a cure now, and I figure it's worth trying because I've got nothing else to lose, but in the village, just living day after day knowing how things were going to eventually end. Knowing I wasn't going to live more than a week, a month, a year maybe...I couldn't take it anymore."

"That's just like life. We could have died any day even if we were normal."

"But I could *feel* it inside me. The change. The symptoms, building under my skin, inside my bones, burning me up, hurting me, affecting my life every moment of every day. I could feel death coming. Inevitable. Inescapable."

"That's why you didn't plan to leave. You *actually* wanted to die. You're worse than I was."

"I don't know if there is a worse and a better," she said. "Maybe I just wanted some control too. We're both going to die anyway."

He stopped. "There's a cure."

She made to move past him and continue but he blocked her.

"There is," he insisted.

She wanted to fight with him about it. It wasn't fair that he had given her hope. But at the same time maybe the hope was real. Maybe there *was* a cure. If there was a cure then she could live, and all this worry about death would be time wasted. She almost cried at the thought. Living would be worth it. A future was worth it. Then the anxieties of the past wouldn't matter. Could be forgotten. She nodded. When he turned away she felt tears on her cheeks despite her best efforts to contain them.

"We should stop soon," he said after a while. "We need to find a good spot to sleep while it's still light."

THEY STOPPED IN A small clearing where they could safely light a bigger fire. The boy built up a rough ring of rocks and went off to gather materials. The girl wondered if he could find them an animal to eat, even if it was already dead, like the ones he had gathered on the island. The thought of the dead things didn't sicken her anymore. All she could think of was her hunger. In the end she didn't ask. He built the fire and didn't offer.

She opened his bag and took out the remaining food. It wasn't a lot. The cure had to be close or they would run out. They were probably going to run out tonight.

"We might have to find a road," she said. "Find some people, and some food."

"Maybe," the boy responded.

Soon the fire burned high—they decided it didn't matter how big it was as long as they didn't burn the forest down, so they built it big—and the sky grew dark. The forest was frightening in the early night time. It was frightening during the day in its vastness—in its obvious power to swallow them and never let them go—but at night the leaves threw shadows that shifted as clouds moved over the moon. Shadows that seemed to creep and crawl and grow, then recede. Waiting. The girl moved closer to the boy in her unease.

"What are you afraid of?" he asked when he noticed how close she was. "We're the monsters here."

She looked him over and wondered why she wasn't afraid of him. She was a so-called monster but he had killed a person. Maybe it was the fact that he had dared her, with his eyes. When she had thought him a monster for killing animals, he had dared her to be afraid and she had stared back and refused. He had dared her, until she mentioned the dead man. Maybe that was the reason she trusted him. She studied his eyes now in the fading light. They glinted with reflected fire, becoming monstrous through the transformation.

"I'm not used to the trees," she said.

"They're unsettling, aren't they. The mainland is quiet and immense, with no one and nothing around."

A bird called in the growing darkness.

"The birds are here," she said.

The boy smiled. His smile was nice, though crooked. His unnaturally sharp teeth reminded the girl of her own. She looked away.

They shared the remainder of the food between them and drank more of the water than they probably should have. When they lay down to sleep, the forest filled with the sounds of animals and the girl drew even closer to the boy in the dark. Her body ached after the walking and with the new growths that plagued her. The pain kept her awake.

She had finally started to fall asleep when an owl screamed. The eerie sound echoed off the closed-in canopy. The boy stirred beside her. He sat up next to the fire, his bare arms exposed to the night as his coat slid off him. He looked back at her, checking if she was awake. She shifted, propping herself up slightly to watch him.

"This one has been bothering me all day." He ran his fingers along a ridge on his left arm. There was a visible pattern of feathers there, just under the skin. "It hurts, and it itches."

His fingers stopped. He must have found a spot where a small feather broke his skin. A scab-like bump. She had them too.

He lifted the edge of it with a nail and expertly pulled it out. She didn't flinch or look away when he did. The motion was so practiced and so unlike her technique that she was mesmerised. He dropped the feather in the fire.

That made her sit up. There hadn't been much more in the fire at the shore when they escaped the island. But this fire was tall and its smoke dispersed above them. She waited to see if anything would happen. Animals called all around them. The day birds were silent now, but the owl hooted again. Smoke swirled into the moonlit sky.

The fire needed more. The girl joined the boy. The arm was a good place to take growths from. She had feathers there, and some bone shards near her wrist that made it look inhuman. She hated them the most. Such an important joint—the wrist. So hard to hide. She pressed on her skin until she felt one. Then, finding her nails long and sharp, grown quickly on their journey, she pressed one into her skin and dug out a shard of bone. It slid into her hand in a gush of blood. The boy watched without disgust, understanding in his eyes.

She dropped it into the fire and the spray of blood caused a wave of smoke that blew over them and entered her lungs. The world slowed. They sat in that stillness and quiet for a moment, thoughts swirling just beyond reach.

"Should we try the ash?" the girl asked. "Better to find out what it does now than when we need it."

The boy appraised her with reflective eyes, then he went to his bag and brought back the packet with the ash from their first fire. He opened it and tapped some of the sooty powder onto his palm. He pushed it around in his hand, then brought it to his face and breathed it in. He coughed and sneezed while the girl did the same.

Almost immediately the girl felt the boy's mind beside hers. It filled the empty sky and drifted with the smoke. Into the branches above—the trees grown from the earth that was made of the bodies of the things that had lived on it. Into the clouds that passed—in the drops of water condensing above that would form rain that held pieces of the bodies of those who made up the earth.

The girl fell back on the grass. The boy did the same and she rolled over until she looked into his eyes and he looked into hers. They looked until they looked inside each other. The earth hummed against the girl, power flowing through it, from deep below. She rejected it and looked back at the boy. Only at the boy.

The night wasn't frightening anymore, but it was filled with pain. The boy's pain matched the girl's. She saw it in his mind. She felt it in his body. It seeped from him, as it did from her. The night was also full of sound. The animals hidden beyond the ring of light screamed at them, knowing what the boy had done to the man on the island, knowing how the two of them had come to be there. Knowing their pain. Knowing no one could live with that pain for long. Seeing death in their future.

The girl and the boy didn't speak aloud, but they communicated. The boy pushed their pain at the animals in the night, pushing them away from the fire, pushing them away from the clearing which now belonged to monsters. To make it safe for monsters. But the girl pulled them back in. The boy's questioning mind asked why. Hers tried to answer.

She didn't want the animals to have their pain. She didn't want anyone to feel such pain. She wanted the boy to leave his mutating body and escape into the animals of the forest. Feel the world as they did. Free. Strong. Alive. She wanted it for herself too. To think only of life. Of how to live. Each moment, each minute, each day. With no fear or knowledge of the impending death the girl had foreseen since the first time she found a feather in her skin.

Her mind went to the owl that screeched in the darkness. And she could see like the owl. See the tiny movements below that meant food. That meant life. She could fly like her, and take those tiny lives to prolong her own. The owl was death. All the animals that called in the night were the same. They were life and death and life again. She stretched her perfect wings in a flurry of excitement and joy.

The boy went to a wolf who was death lurking near the edge of the clearing. Who watched them while slumped down, seeming at ease but very alert. The wolf howled into the night at the strangeness of the intrusion but eventually let him in. The boy looked into the trees with the wolf's strong night eyes and saw a great dark owl in their branches, her mighty wings spread. The two animals shared a thought.

The girl fell asleep, holding the boy to her. Her mind floated in the smoke from the fire, straying from her damaged body and this time—instead of a brutal nightmare of murder in a town square—she dreamed of the freedom of a pain-free existence in the mind of an owl who knew what she was, and didn't care.

THE NEXT MORNING THEY trudged on. The girl's boots had never fully dried despite being placed by the fire each night. They would seem dry, feeling only cold—difficult to distinguish from damp—and yet moisture would inevitably leak out as she walked and chafe her feet and ankles. Under the chaffing skin and growing blisters there were bones that shouldn't be there. They cut from the inside and her boots filled with blood, wetting them anew.

The forest felt endless. It went on in every direction and there didn't seem to be a break in it. The girl had started to realise just how impossible it might be to find the meadow that held the cure. It had seemed a simple journey, but it was long and it all looked the same.

The boy soldiered on ahead of her, his steps slightly staggered. Pain was written in his right stride cut shorter than his left, in the awkward stiffness of one of his arms. He turned his whole body to look back at her instead of just his head. His neck must feel like hers.

"I think I see a road," he said.

The girl squinted through the trees and couldn't see a change. She followed him and as they grew closer she finally saw the slight break in the trunks. It framed a muddy path. Not much of a road, but at least a sign of people. She held back when she recognised it. People meant danger.

But people might also mean food and water, and directions.

It was unlikely they could find the meadow on their own. Not when the forest was so big. Bigger than their entire island. And who's to say the walk wasn't weeks long instead of days? They couldn't survive that. They were almost out of water already and they had nothing left to eat.

The boy waited by the side of the road for her. She joined him tentatively and looked in both directions.

"We should walk along it," he said.

"It'll be dangerous."

The look he gave her said he'd considered the danger already and dismissed it. Was it an echo of his actual thoughts she heard or just a deeper understanding of *him* she had gained since they became partners on this journey? Regardless, they needed help. Even if they didn't find anyone, if the Black Mage with the cure lived anywhere near civilization, this road might take them there.

"We'll cover ourselves completely," he said. "No one can tell from your face."

It still wasn't safe, but the girl had to agree they needed the road.

"We'll continue south along it until it changes direction," the boy said. "Then we'll take stock and decide what to do. It looks well travelled. If we see people we can judge whether it's safe to ask for help or not."

"Alright." The girl looked in the direction they would go. No one there yet. "Let's try it."

The road travelled south-south-east, if the girl had to guess. It might take them slightly out of their way but it was easier going than the untamed forest floor. The rough path beneath her feet made the girl daydream of a ride in a plush carriage that led to a soft bed to spend the night in. The boy might be used to roughing it—out on the farm, sleeping on the heath with the sheep—but she wasn't.

Such a sheltered life she had lived. She'd ridden horses with her brothers, or run in the fields just to feel what her body could do—or she had before the change. She'd planted an herb garden in her courtyard and tended it until she got bored. But that was it. The extent of her minor hardships. All more fun than work. Now she trudged cross-country in a place she didn't know and slept on rocks and dirt, every part of her body aching with the effort and the change.

The clopping of a horse trotting up the road roused her from her musings.

"Someone's coming."

A wagon appeared between the trees behind them, travelling in the same direction they walked. One horse pulled it and a man sat at the front directing it. The girl shrugged her coat up higher, close to her ears, and made sure her hair fanned out to cover her neck. The boy put up his hood.

"I say we ask for directions," he said.

"It must be a busy road," she responded. "It has to be for us to see someone so quickly. We should judge each passer before we speak to them."

"What if there isn't another? We need help."

She was going to argue when the wagon caught up and their choice was made for them.

"Hello there!" the man in the seat bellowed. "What are you two doing walking way out here?"

The boy exchanged a glance with the girl as the wagon came to a stop. Again she wondered if she felt a whisper of his thoughts. She knew what he was going to say before he said it.

"We were shipwrecked on the beach," the boy said. "In the storm two days ago. We were walking inland to find someone who could tell us exactly where we are. Best to head south, we figured."

"Where did your ship come from that you don't know where you are?" The man remained seated, holding the horse's reins. His posture wasn't threatening, but the question was pointed.

"We're from the island," the girl said.

"Ah," the man replied. "I'm not surprised. It was a bad storm. Water in the channel gets choppy. If you hop in the back I can take you up the road to the nearest village."

The girl and the boy exchanged another look before the boy led the way around the cart to the back. He lifted himself easily onto the crates secured there, showing none of his previous stiffness and pain, covering it well, and offered the girl a hand up. She took it and sat in front of the boy, looking toward the man who was driving. He watched them until they settled then turned back to his horse. The top of the back of his head was balding.

"So you came from the island," the man said as he got the horse walking again. "Not the best season to be out in the boats. Especially not with the orcas coming through."

"It was a bad harvest last year," the boy answered. "We were sent for supplies."

Good answer. They could never have passed as fisher-people.

The man was silent for a moment. Then he seemed to relax. The girl worried about that lapse. The boy didn't seem concerned and he slouched against the edge of the wagon bed, letting his hood fall back and raising his chin to the filtered sunlight that sifted through the trees, his tired muscles resting. He smiled at her. It was better than walking.

"You said there's a village up the road?" the boy asked.

"Not far by wagon. Would have taken you a few hours to walk."

"Anything else around here?"

"Not really."

"The forest is quite big," the boy continued. "We don't have trees like this on the island. We can see the sky in all directions. Here everything is closed in."

The girl raised an eyebrow at the boy. He smirked.

"There's a big meadow on the way to the village," the man said. "Huge break in the trees."

"Is it far from here?"

The man looked back at them, turning his eyes down on the boy, and the girl noticed how he studied him. She met the boy's eyes and he turned to the man, who turned away to the road.

"It's just along this road," the man said when he faced forward.

The boy smiled again, relaxed, happy to have brought them within reach of the meadow and his promised cure. The girl smiled back. She took his hand, running a finger over his sharp nails, then covered them by holding his hand in her lap.

She leaned back, gazing into the bright green canopies of the spring trees as the wagon bumped down the muddy path. The rocking hurt her but not as much as walking would have. She wondered what the villages on the mainland looked like. Probably much like their own on the island. Maybe they could find a place in this one, as long as no one discovered them before they could be cured.

The girl's head lolled sleepily as they crossed a more uniform section of road, the rhythmic knocking of the crates and the wagon bed lulling her into a stupor. She opened her eyes on and off, shafts of piercing sunlight breaking through her lids. The man looked back at her once and she smiled drowsily. He looked down at the boy whose eyes were closed and whose coat slid to the side.

The wagon stopped. The girl roused herself and found the boy waking as well. He only had time to furrow his brow before the man turned suddenly and cracked him across the back of the head.

The girl opened her eyes wide and felt frozen, fear prickling her skin. The horse screamed and bucked, shaking the wagon, but the man soothed it.

"Came from the island in the early spring with a girl on the boat," he said when it was calm. "Looking for the meadow where the Black Mage lives. Must have heard the rumours of a cure."

The boy lay doubled over in the wagon bed. Out cold. He should heal quickly from that hit, but he didn't move at all. The girl couldn't leave him.

"He your sweetheart?" The man pushed the boy's coat collar down to reveal the growths on the back of his neck. "Can't blame a girl for protecting her young lover but you should know he has to die. He'd only have killed you when he turned."

He shook the boy by the shoulder, menacing the club he must have struck with, but didn't hit again. "Maybe the Black Mage will pay for his body. I'd give you a piece of it, to help you start your life over. It really should be yours." The man looked up at her and frowned at her wide-eyed stare. "You must have known."

The girl continued to stare. She tried to speak but nothing came out.

The man's eyes narrowed. "You're one too, aren't ya?"

The girl turned and leapt off the back of the wagon, the creak and shake of the man's weight shifting on it as he rose to follow reverberating through her feet when they left the wood. She ran a few staggering steps down the road. Hesitated. Nearly turned back for the boy. A crack sounded and sharp pain blinded her as blazing lights grew in front of her eyes.

SHE WOKE SLUMPED AGAINST the side of the wagon. The pain in her head made her wince and there was a ringing in her ears. The boy was propped up beside her, unmoving. Her hands were bound behind her back. Too strong a tie to be undone. She struggled against the bite of the rope for a moment, her straining muscles screaming, before giving up. Then she noticed muddied boots in her peripheral vision. The man stood in the road. The girl writhed against her bindings and cried.

The horse neighed and snorted indignantly and the man went to placate it. The girl turned to the boy as best she could and tried to nudge him awake.

"Please," she said. "Please wake up."

He didn't move. Was he dead? No, no, he couldn't be dead. She cried against his hair and thought she heard a low groan. She pushed his head with her shoulder and he gasped and looked up. His dark, reflective eyes were unfocused at first but quickly became clear. He must be healing fast.

"What can we do?" she asked.

He shook his head slowly. The man came around the wagon, passing them and jumping up in the back. The boy didn't move but his eyes followed the man. He didn't speak but the girl saw his worry, or sensed it. No access to fire. No access to blood unless it dripped over their faces enough to be consumed. This was the end. There was no hope now.

The girl cried quietly. The boy was stoic and didn't move, his breath hot against her skin.

"Wait," she whispered. "Blood."

The boy's eyes came slowly back to hers.

"Bite me," she said quietly.

The man's heavy footfalls thudded in the girl's ringing ears. Then she felt the sharp cut of the boy's teeth in her shoulder. The man shouted and wrestled her to her feet with one hand as he brandished his club in the other, threatening the boy where he lay on the ground. The boy's mouth brimmed with dark blood. Too dark. Monster blood.

"Maybe I should kill you now," the man said. "No reason for the Black Mage to want you alive."

The girl felt a mild pounding in the ground and thought it was her heart before she heard the clip of horses hooves. Another wagon came up the road towards them. The man cursed and carried her back to the wagon bed.

"Help!" she screamed as the second wagon came into view. She probably couldn't hide what she was but if she could involve the man with newcomers it might grant them time. "Help us!"

The second wagon pulled up and a younger man stepped off it.

"What's going on here then?" he asked gruffly.

The man threw the girl on top of the crates and went to address the newcomer. A young woman waited silently on the other wagon seat, her gaze averted.

"He attacked us," the girl said in her direction, pleading. "My husband is bloodied in the road from his club. You have to help us."

The two men spoke. The girl heard the word "monsters" over the sound of the horse's disgruntled whinny. Then the boy appeared from behind the wagon. He must have broken the rope that tied his hands because he walked unencumbered, stealthily approaching.

The young woman with the other wagon screamed and their horse reared but it was too late. The boy took their captor from behind and with his bare hands he broke the man's neck. The girl turned away at the sharp snap, closing her eyes and feeling her heart beat throughout her body. The newcomer shouted and she heard a scuffle.

The girl opened her eyes and threw herself out of the wagon, staggering towards the two. She shouted at the boy to stop and he did. The newcomer didn't move. His neck and chest were slashed where the boy's clawed fingers had raked him. The boy stood and turned his attention to her. He undid the bonds that held her while the young woman screamed and cried from the other wagon seat, her horse snorting and shaking in its harness.

The first man was clearly dead. The newcomer—likely husband or brother or cousin to the young woman—lay injured in the dirt. The girl stared down at him as the boy tried to get her to leave.

"No," she said. "He stopped to help us."

"But what can we do for him?"

"You said we could heal."

"I don't know if that will work."

"It's worth a try, isn't it?"

The woman finally attempted to run away when the girl approached. "Tie her with the rope that held me," she said to the boy. He caught the young woman easily and held her still.

"We're going to help him," the girl said, indicating the man on the ground. His breathing was heavy and he didn't move. Blood gushed from him, red and natural. Human. "You'll need to be here for him when he wakes. In return you will answer some questions about this place."

The girl nodded to the boy to begin asking while she knelt to create a liniment. Ground bones and blood, she figured. Blood was easy. Bones were harder. She opened the bag the boy had given her and found the mortar and pestle at the bottom.

She rolled up her sleeve and cut her arm around the wrist, where the most accessible bone shards were. Blood poured into the mortar at an alarming rate but she wasn't worried. The cut would heal quickly. She felt around for a free shard of bone that shouldn't be there and came up with two. One was keen and splintered and one was round and flat. She pressed them out and dropped them in the mortar with the blood. She took the pestle in her stiffening fingers and began to grind them down.

The living man groaned behind her. The dead man observed the strange scene with sightless eyes. When the liniment was smooth enough to spread the girl returned to the boy.

"And the Black Mage lives there?" he asked.

"On a compound in the meadow." The young woman whimpered. "Please just leave us be."

"He might not live if we leave him like that." The girl walked to the boy with the mortar. "Your head."

The gash from the club hadn't completely healed. She wasn't going to try the liniment on a stranger first. It had to be on the boy. He nodded, knowing what she wanted.

She took a bit of the bloody paste on her fingers and gently smoothed it over the laceration in the boy's scalp, covering the bleeding wound, mixing her dark blood with his. When she wiped the wet paste away the wound had closed, like magic. A hideous scar was left in its place.

Hopefully it would work on a human as well as it did on a monster.

She moved to the injured man and poured the liniment onto his neck and chest, smoothing it into the edges of the cuts. It seemed to stop the bleeding, the red flow parting and turning black and stagnant, but she figured it could take a while to heal him, since he wasn't a monster himself.

"There," she said to the woman. "He'll be fine now."

The boy released her from the rope he had tied her with and she screamed at his touch.

"We're not really monsters," the girl said, but the boy pulled her away.

"I found food and water in the wagon," he said. "The meadow isn't far from here but the trees are sparse and the ground is flat so we could take the horses. I assume you can ride. We need to get off this road before someone else sees us."

The young woman knelt in the dirt, holding her injured companion. The girl didn't think it was fair to take their horse.

"We only need one horse if it isn't far."

The boy glanced at the newcomers in their state of distress and seemed to agree. He ran to the horse that had pulled the dead man's wagon. Maybe he approached too quickly or maybe it was his monstrous scent but the animal's eyes rolled up in its head, whites showing. It bared its teeth at him and emitted a high pitched squeal. The girl recognised the aggressive posturing and looked down the road anxiously.

The boy slowed and murmured under his breath, hoping to soothe the startled creature. But even with this, the horse reared in its harness at his approach, screaming, lifting the wagon and dropping it with a crack.

"It's too cruel." The girl put a hand on the boy's shoulder and drew him away. "They must not like monsters."

"Or murderers."

The horse stared at them and snorted.

"She said it wasn't far," the boy said with false enthusiasm. "Come on, we'll continue on foot."

The girl let him lead her, leaving the corpse in the road with his angry horse, the sobbing woman, and the healing man. As they disappeared into the trees the girl looked back and saw the newcomer sit up gasping. She almost smiled but her body hurt too much. She turned away and followed the boy.

THE EDGE OF THE forest had approached like a dream in the night. Staring into the meadow the entire dark sky was visible again, from the horizon up to the moon and back down to the tops of their heads. The girl was happy to see it. She stood looking at the seemingly endless field of grass for too long, as if frozen. The frantic energy of the escape had faded and now she had nothing left.

The last leg of their walk had been the hardest. It would have been quicker with the horse but probably more painful, and treacherous in the growing dark. The boy's growths had seemed to torture him, too deep and extensive to be removed on the go. He had staggered on ahead of the girl as if only half-alive. The girl had watched him, partly afraid he would also lose his mind to the pain, to the transformation. Now that they were safe again she couldn't forget how he had twisted the bad man's head on his neck. The sharp snap when the spine had broken.

Of course the boy could snap a man's neck. He had killed the blacksmith, she reminded herself. He was a murderer before the wagon. She had to remind herself that she knew all this already and had still travelled with him for all this time. Just because she had seen it now didn't mean anything had changed. This was nothing new. He would never hurt her. She didn't believe he could.

She continued to stand and stare into the meadow until the boy collapsed to his knees beside her. The girl knelt to check him and found herself slowed by the pain as well. The walk had been hard, but she had continued it by thinking of how it would only last so long and then it would end. She had known there wasn't far to go and she had been able to convince herself to continue because of that. Perhaps the boy had been the same.

"We should stop here tonight." The boy's voice was quiet and she felt the agony in it.

The girl sat beside him for a moment, relishing the feel of not standing, not walking. Then she forced herself to get up and build a small fire. She set it using the flint and steel from the bag and came back to the boy to find he hadn't moved.

"The Black Mage is out there somewhere," he said. "Like my father told me. Like the mainlanders confirmed."

"We'll look in the morning. It's too dark now and we need to rest."

"There's a cure, right? There has to be."

The girl wasn't sure if she should answer. She hadn't imagined there was a cure on her own. Not before she found out what she was, and not after she knew. She'd believed herself dead as soon as her transformation began. The idea of a cure had come from the boy. When he saved the girl and told her why. *He* had brought them to this place. How could he doubt now?

"I think there must be," she said. "I think your father heard those stories for a reason and he told them to you because he wanted you to have a chance. I'm thankful you chose to save me to give me that same chance."

The boy's eyes looked liquid in the light of the fire. He didn't answer.

The crunch of the man's neck came back to the girl. She shut her eyes to shut it out. But she also remembered the man brutally striking the boy across the skull, the look in his eyes when he realised the girl was the same. The moment he said he would kill them. That man had been a monster. They had never threatened him. Never would have harmed him if he hadn't attacked them. In killing him, the boy had simply saved them both again.

She reached for the boy in the darkness, finding his cheek with her clumsy fingers. She turned his face to hers and leaned down to kiss him. He responded immediately, pulling her against him and rolling her over in the grass. She felt his eagerness to be with her, but she also felt him flinch out of it as the changes inside his body grated at the rapid movements. He froze on top of her, their kiss harsh and stiff.

He pulled away, lifting himself enough to meet her eyes.

"I could still do it," she said. "If you want to."

She was in pain, but that was life. Even more, it was her life. Had been for years. He ran his fingers down her neck and over her chest but his eyes told her it wasn't going to happen. The unsteadiness of his arm worried her.

"When we're cured then," she said.

He slumped down beside her and she could tell it took all his strength not to collapse on top of her. He rolled to the side and looked at the sky. She joined him. The stars were visible again, above the empty meadow, like they had been on the raft at sea. She remembered the great eye that had winked at them. Perhaps she would see it again.

"You're so beautiful," the boy said. "I didn't really look at you back home because I never could have imagined."

"You could have."

He laughed and stopped when the movement must have hurt him. It ended in a choked cough. "Well, maybe I imagined a little. But, well, you know."

"You're not exactly what my parents would have wanted for me."

"They didn't want you settling down with a monster? That's surprising."

She laughed and knew why he had stopped. There was something growing in her chest now, constricting her breath. It hurt. It was frightening.

She took his hand in hers and rubbed her thumb over his palm. Rough. Monster hands. But they must have been rough before from working on the farm. So different from hers. She rubbed her other thumb over her own palm and was disturbed by what she felt. Her skin was getting tougher too. It felt like it belonged to someone else. The boy's nails were long and sharp now. Hers weren't far behind.

"We're going to be okay," she said, feeling his pulse. "We're changing but our hearts are still human."

She held his hand against her chest and at the same time she put her other hand on his.

"Our hearts," he said.

"Hold onto this. Still alive. Still human."

He moved closer to her, and his warmth and the warmth of the fire lulled her into a kind of trance. It wasn't exactly pain-free but it was better than anything she had felt in a long time.

THE GIRL WOKE TO someone nudging her with a boot. She wanted to spring up, ready to run if needed, but she struggled to move at all. Her body was a mass of pain. The boy lay against her back. Immobile. Cold. She turned over as quickly as she could in fear, to check him. She was worried, but as she shifted he groaned.

"Well, they're alive."

The girl's attention was drawn to the person who spoke. Two people stood in the meadow before them. Two women, it looked like. The one who had nudged the girl stood over them and studied them. The other stood back with her hands in her pockets.

"What are you doing here?" the other asked.

The boy groaned again. The girl tried to wake him but he only moaned and twitched.

"Is he okay?" the first woman asked.

The girl was in so much pain and the boy was catatonic. She didn't know what she could possibly do at this point. The boy had wanted to live, but what kind of life was this? If these women found out what the girl and the boy were they might kill them, but was there really any other option at this point? The girl might be able to go on, but the boy wasn't going anywhere like this, and she couldn't carry him. She couldn't leave him either.

"We're looking for the Black Mage," the girl said. "The one who lives in the meadow."

The women exchanged a glance.

"What do you want with a Black Mage?" the first woman asked.

The girl almost cried. The pain and the decision loomed over her. Then she saw the woman who was farther back examining the boy. A portion of his bare arm was exposed, the dark shadows of hidden feathers clearly visible. The girl rushed to cover it, the growing tears breaking over her lids as she did. The woman's eyes grew wide.

The girl didn't have the strength to fight like they had fought the man with the wagon. She pulled the boy close, waiting. She hadn't known him well but he had saved her, and he was the only one who cared about her now. She buried her face in his coat and he mumbled against her, his words nonsense, his body cold. She waited for a blow, or a piercing cut. For the end.

But what she got instead was the woman's gentle hand on her shoulder. She looked up.

The woman pulled back her sleeve to expose white scarring. "You're here for the cure."

The girl dissolved into tears.

THE GIRL HOBBLED INTO the main building of the compound behind a large man who carried the boy over his shoulder. The boy screamed inhumanly and arched against the man's back, but the man bore his weight like he was nothing.

He was a frightening man. Huge. Silent. He hadn't said a word since one of the two women brought him to carry the boy. The girl had thought he might be the Black Mage when he arrived, but none of the three strangers had yet exposed themselves as such.

A third woman stood in the centre of the high-ceilinged room. She appeared to be much younger than the others. This woman was dressed in a long black cloak that wrapped around her body and closed in the front. She wore thick black gloves over her hands that reached to her elbows. A hood was stretched over her head to cover her hair and put her face in shadow, even though they were inside. The young woman looked out from her deep hood with piercing blue eyes.

"Two of you at once?" she said quietly. "Interesting."

The big man carried the boy through a door, into an interior room, leaving the girl where she stood. The young woman studied her.

"You have more time than he does," she said, "but not much more. I will have to operate on both of you today if there is any chance for you to be saved."

The two older women waited silently to the side of the room. They stared at the young woman with an almost religious obsession.

"You're the Black Mage," the girl said.

The Black Mage nodded. The girl frowned. The Black Mage looked to be not much older than she and the boy. Perhaps five years older at most. It didn't make sense with the stories the boy's father had heard and passed on to him. The Black Mage must have been healing monsters for years for the stories of her deeds to spread as far as the island. The two other women were older though. If one of them had been healed near the age of the girl and the boy, it had to have been at least ten years ago. Maybe the Black Mage only looked young. Maybe she stayed that way by the dark magic she performed. The blood magic. Or maybe she had started as an apprentice. The new Black Mage in the meadow.

"I must go to your friend now. Please wait here. It shouldn't be long. Then I will work on you."

The Black Mage looked to the two women at the wall.

"Bring her food and water, please. There is nothing that can be done for the boy until I have worked, but this one can be prepared better."

The Black Mage left through the door the big man had taken. The boy's piercing screams grew loud, but the heavy wooden door muffled them again when it closed behind the Black Mage. The women brought food and water for the girl. She tried to drink slowly and savour the soft bread rather than stuff it all in her mouth at once.

There was something strange about the women and the big man. The two women stood motionless at the edge of the room and stared into space while the girl ate. They had seemed normal in the meadow but as they'd approached the compound their eyes had changed and they ceased to speak. The big man had been like that since he arrived, but the change in the women was marked. Since entering the main building the Black Mage had been the only one of the four of them who had expressions outside blank and adoration.

The girl thought she heard the boy cry out a few times, but mostly there was silence. When the Black Mage returned the girl considered that they might have just killed the boy. Maybe it was all a trick. She felt a moment of nausea and almost lost the food and water she'd consumed. But the first woman's scars had looked real—had looked like the scarring on the girl's arm from their fight with the sea. And the girl remembered the state she had been in at the edge of the forest. At least she was warm now, and her stomach was full. She almost understood the adoration on the women's faces at that thought. If she had to die, at least now she was more comfortable.

"Come with me," the Black Mage said.

The big man joined them and led the girl into the second room. The boy wasn't there, but there were more doors in the other walls leading farther into the building. They must have taken him somewhere else. The girl considered asking but didn't see much difference at that point. She would live or she would die. If the pain ended, she didn't care.

"Your friend is in the other room, recovering," the Black Mage said, likely seeing the concern on the girl's face.

The girl nodded. A wide table with straps in the middle of it stood in the centre of the room, with a smaller surface at its side, covered in an array of evil looking tools. As the girl approached she noticed dark streaks on the floor around the table, as if blood had been hastily cleaned. She averted her eyes. The Black Mage had said it was an operation. Of course there would be blood.

The girl took in the rest of the room to occupy her mind. There were three doors and one window. In the wall-space unoccupied by the doors and window there were shelves displaying various sized beakers and glass jars full of dark and gruesome things. Closed cupboards filled the rest of the available space, hiding their contents from the girl's curious eyes.

The big man indicated the girl should lie on the table. Then he left the room.

"Undress," the Black Mage said.

The girl looked at the young woman warily but did as she asked, leaving her dirty man's clothing in a pile on the floor and lying down on one side of the table. The Black Mage lifted straps from under the edge of it to secure one of the girl's arms and legs. She did the same on the other side with the straps from the centre of the table. The dark shadows of things that didn't belong were more prominent now, extra bones and feathers jutted out as the girl shifted her weight in the restraints. The pain of them made her gasp.

"I will remove the growths," the Black Mage said. "All of them at once, before you can heal. That's the only way to cure it."

The Black Mage secured the girl tightly. The restraints were uncomfortable but the girl had to imagine the tension was necessary. The feel of the foreign parts in her body was worse. The Black Mage moved to the edge of the table and examined her.

"You should take this." She held out a small beaker half-full of dark liquid. "The operation will hurt even with pain relief, but this is the best I can do for you. The surgery will be easier on you than it was on your friend because there is less to remove, but you will wish you were in his state of delirium once I start."

The girl drank the liquid the Black Mage held to her lips and immediately felt numbed. It made her sleepy, and the existing pain dulled. She closed her eyes and gritted her teeth, anticipating the new pain. She still wasn't sure if this was the cure or if she would die, but hope bloomed inside her—numbed like the rest of her body, but there. Hope bloomed as blood bloomed from her skin, as the Black Mage began to cut.

The girl screamed at the thought of what was being done to her, more than at the pain of it. Her imagination knew what was happening to her even if her drugged body did not.

ANIMALS RAN THROUGH THE girl's mind and before her eyes. They ran with joy in every movement, without pain and full of life. But as the girl looked closer she realised the animals were dying. Their skin and fur hung free of their bodies and blew in the wind streaming over them. Their muscles rotted off and their bones ground against each other until they fell apart.

They dropped to the earth, one by one, no longer joyous, no longer hale. Their remains screamed as they were trampled by the others, others who decayed and fell apart themselves as they crushed the dead ones beneath their dying feet. The tide of death swept towards her and then the girl was under it, being crushed with the rest. Her own flesh rotted off her body in front of her eyes and her bones were ground to dust.

She woke screaming.

She was hot. Hot as the summer sun. Her skin should stream sweat but instead it was dry. Agonising pain ripped through her. The boy was there, blurry, at the edge of the bed where she lay. She saw the questions on his face. He looked fine. Pain free. Feather free. Shadow free. He frowned at her as she writhed against his touch, his face normal one moment and a mask of shadows the next.

"What's wrong?" His voice echoed and created a reverberation in her mind that threatened to drive her mad.

She was dying. She had to be.

"What's wrong with her?"

The boy disappeared from the side of the bed. The girl moved her head slowly, painfully to find him, to follow him across the room as he left through the open door and demanded of the two silent women why the girl was not recovering when he was fine. The three of them moved haltingly, and they came in and out of the girl's altered vision as they danced a disordered drama.

The girl looked around the room and found a window. She tried to focus on the streams of light coming in. Flashes of the tide of dead animals from her fevered sleep invaded her waking vision and her pain drove her out of her mind and into theirs.

A great stag with maggoty holes for eyes appeared behind the window panes. It flew through the glass, not breaking it, the points on its majestic antlers bursting through the wall. It hovered before her. A spectre. Its maw opened as if to speak but its lower jaw cracked and fell to the floor instead. The girl tried to move away to escape the sight but her body was numb and didn't respond to her wailing mind. The stag hovered there, with half a face, and came no closer.

The cure was no cure. Not for the girl. Instead it was a death sentence. Yet, the boy might live. The girl struggled to focus on him as he walked back and forth in the room, through the stag, shouting, fighting for her. He would survive. He would go on. She was happy about that.

He came back to her. He sat beside the bed and blocked the dead stag from her view. He held her hand and it hurt. She was too weak to draw back so she let him. He cried silently.

"There must be something I can do," he said. "I brought you here to be cured, not to die. You look fine. You look like me. There's nothing wrong with you!"

The girl tried to smile at him but he wasn't looking. He looked at the window. He must see the stag too. The beast looked back at him and she thought it smiled for her, though it no longer had a true mouth. Then the boy moved quickly. Too quickly for her slow eyes to see. A flash of reflection from the spring light filled her vision.

"Here," he said. "We have to try it."

He extended a bloodied arm towards her. Was it red blood? It was still dark to the girl's eyes, but maybe not as dark as it had been. Real blood. She widened her eyes at the sight. What was he doing? He had done the injury to himself. The flash of light had been a knife. But why do this, if he was cured? What could the blood of a boy who was no longer a monster do for her?

He offered her the blood that his heart pumped from his arm and she put her lips against his skin. She wouldn't refuse him the right to try. His warm blood was metalic. She was reminded of the raft in the raging sea. The stag screamed across the room from her and its lower jaw lifted off the floor and grew back into its face.

The girl drank and drank and the boy held her. The wound in his arm closed beneath her tongue, the flesh knitting together thread by thread like writhing worms. Recombining. Reunited. But it shouldn't have. It shouldn't have healed at all, not for days.

It scared her, but she felt better. The heat evaporated from her skin like the sweat that had never come and her head cleared. The stag turned with a screech and faded as it leapt back through the window. The girl nuzzled against the boy's arm and drank no more.

The boy leaned back and studied her, surprise and happiness in his eyes. She managed a smile and cried happy tears against his shirt as the pain subsided under a haze of blood power. She didn't mention that he must not be cured if he could heal her. He must not be.

Not really.

THE GIRL FOLLOWED THE boy into the great greening grasses of the meadow. Spring was evident there, much more so than it would have been on the island at the same time, much more so than it had been at the edge of the mainland only a couple weeks ago when they arrived.

The boy took her hand and led her farther from the Black Mage's building and the memory of what had been done to them. He pulled her quickly across the windswept grass. There was no pain evident in him now, not now that he had mostly healed from the Black Mage's surgery. From the cure.

They had been given small huts to themselves after the procedure. A few stood empty behind the main building. The Black Mage's aids lived in the others. The shelter, as well as food and clean water, was provided to the girl and boy in return for future work around the compound, expected from them once they were fully healed.

They had improved amazingly quickly, once the girl recovered from the mysterious illness that had plagued her. It hadn't been long before she'd been able to leave her bed and sit outside. To enjoy the warming spring air. To walk. Maybe soon to run.

The boy smiled back at the girl. He was carefree and happy. She tried to enjoy her revitalised, pain-free body, but the inconsistencies still bothered her.

She wasn't fully convinced they were cured, but they didn't look like monsters anymore. The strange growths were gone, and the pain and stiffness were gone with them. They were left with scars, but even those seemed to be fading. The girl looked at her exposed wrist as she followed the boy and found that the scars there were nearly gone. It was strange that the first woman who had shown them her scar from being healed still had such vivid marks. White scars, old scars, but still clearly scars. It made the girl wonder if the woman had been cured properly, and if the girl and boy had not been.

"It feels amazing, doesn't it?" the boy said.

He ran his free hand through the tall grass as they walked. He let go of her and ran, laughing, ahead of her.

She put aside her worries and chased him. It had been so long since she felt free. Trapped by her changing body in the village, not willing to take any risks and run with the other young people. She had been forced to be careful at all times to avoid exposing herself. Now she was pain free and free of eyes that would discover her and consign her to the fate that befell all monsters.

The boy disappeared into the grass ahead of her and she slowed, breathing hard. She pushed aside some tall reeds and was surprised when he jumped on her.

"Oof," she said as he toppled her into the soft grass. The ground was cold. He was warm. "What are you doing?" She laughed, showing she wasn't serious or offended. His hands brushed her ribs and waist roughly and the world grew silent. Her body burned for him.

"Looks like you two are feeling well."

The Black Mage appeared through the reeds, stopping to look down at them in her full black cloak and hood. The gloves that now gave the girl terrifying flashbacks were in their habitual places covering the Black Mage's hands and arms. Strange gloves, to be made so long and cover so much. It wasn't cold enough for them now—or for the obscuring cloak and hood either—but the girl didn't remember the Black Mage removing them during or since the surgery.

Everything about the Black Mage's clothing was strange, but the girl guessed it must be related to her position. The need to keep an air of mystery about her. The Black Mage clasped her gloved hands behind her back and regarded them, lying in the grass. The girl separated herself from the boy and looked back at the woman.

"I'm glad," the Black Mage continued. "It's a waste for so many who are so young to be killed when they could be cured. I'm glad you were able to make your way here."

The boy smiled openly and the girl felt his comfort, his ease. He seemed to accept the cure completely. He would enjoy the time they'd been given without a thought to the contradictions. Pain free. Human. But at great cost. The girl shuddered as the invasive memories of the surgery sent painful spikes through her body.

"Are we truly cured?" she asked.

The Black Mage turned her ice-blue eyes on the girl. They never seemed to express any emotion. They didn't look like living eyes. The girl averted her gaze.

"Of course you are," the Black Mage said when she looked away. "You are free of the transformation and will live normal lives from now on. I only ask that you remain here for a time to pay back some of the good will I have done for you by helping with the general maintenance of the compound. If you are still here when the ground thaws it would be appreciated if you helped with the spring planting."

The girl squeezed the boy's hand.

"It will also allow me to monitor you to make sure I got everything," the Black Mage added.

The girl did meet the Black Mage's eyes then. "Got everything?"

"All material must be removed at once for the cure to be complete."

"But you just said we were cured."

"I believe you are. If, by some great oversight, you are not, I will ensure you are before you leave. The outcome is the same. You will be cured before you leave this place."

The girl rolled her eyes at the boy. Not exactly the same outcome. It left more reason for the girl and boy to stay and help with the farm work. What if the Black Mage hadn't healed them fully in order to keep them at the compound indefinitely? Maybe that had something to do with the older woman's scars.

The girl looked up at the Black Mage again. They did owe her though. The girl hadn't spoken with the young woman at any length since she was healed. Healed and then left to die, it had seemed. But no one had interfered when the boy tried to save her and succeeded. They hadn't been upset at her survival.

"Thank you. I didn't—" the girl's voice broke. "I didn't think we could live anymore. Like that."

The Black Mage's expression remained stoic. "I would do it for anyone." She turned to leave, but paused and looked back once more. "Though I would appreciate it if you stay to help some, at least."

"We will," the boy said.

The Black Mage nodded. "Then enjoy yourselves while you recover. And be careful. You have no open wounds on the surface but that does not necessarily reflect what's inside."

When the woman was gone the boy rolled the girl back into the grass.

"You agreed so easily," the girl said.

"What else do we have to do? I've never been this free in my life. I've never spent weeks in bed 'recovering' from anything. Free food—better food than I've ever had. Clean, cold water. All of it delivered to the door of a space I don't have to share."

"I've had better," the girl said, but there was no conviction in her words.

"You've never had me."

He laughed and she put a hand roughly over his mouth to quiet him.

"We also have nowhere else to go," he added against her palm.

The girl frowned, withdrawing her hand. She missed her family and her home. She felt a pang of sadness at the loss, quickly stamped out by the memories of them attacking her. They weren't her family anymore. The quicker she got over that the better. They didn't care about her. They might even be happy she was gone. Did her mother cry in the night remembering what she had done? Mourning her daughter? They hadn't been close, partly because the girl had rejected closeness in order to hide. Did her father cry? Her brothers? Especially the youngest...

She sat upright, looking down on the boy. He lay back comfortably in the grass. The smile on his face was easy, and his eyes were human. It was the most natural she had seen him since he saved her. And he was right. They had nowhere to go. That was unfortunate, but also freeing. They could work on the Black Mage's farm for as long as they wanted and as long as she would let them stay. Clean water. Reasonable food. It remained to be seen how the work went, but it couldn't be worse than anything the boy had done before. The girl would learn.

They had a future. Decisions to make about it. It was something the girl hadn't been forced to contemplate in a long time. Hadn't been allowed to. The prospect of the years ahead of her settled on her mind and she knew it was time to start figuring things out. She felt grateful to have the boy.

"I guess we're going to live," she said.

He laughed and pulled her to him. "What is this, 'I guess'? We are! We always were. I told you that the night we left the island."

She relaxed in his arms. He was kind and hopeful. He had been a beautiful monster and he was a beautiful boy. All they had were each other now. He drew her closer, pressing his body against hers, his breath soft against her cheek. She turned her head to find his lips brushed hers. Her body thrummed with pleasure, no pain to take away from it. But a thought nagged her.

"I don't think we're cured," she said against his lips.

"Cured enough to do this," he whispered back.

She surrendered to the satisfaction her healed body could give her. The boy clearly did the same. It was easy because she wasn't afraid to show herself to him. All of herself, with all her healing scars, for now she didn't hurt.

Afterwards they lay in the grass together, undisturbed by the others who lived in the meadow. The girl ran her hands over the great swirling scars on the boy's back and traced the raised straight lines of those on his chest. They had faded quickly but they were still extensive and alarming. A normal person could never have survived such an extreme operation.

He pulled her against him again and she sighed. It was so wonderful. To be alive. To live. As she traced the patterns of abused flesh on his back her fingers caught on a scab.

She froze. Stifling heat rose in her as the fear of a failed cure took hold once more. But she forced herself to stop. To calm. It was just a scab. A hallmark of healing. It was not the beginnings of a feather under the skin. Just her imagination. Just her old mind worried that hope was a lie and that nothing would ever get better. She dismissed it. They just hadn't healed perfectly yet.

WARMTH CAME QUICKLY TO the land on the compound, thawing the earth and preparing it to grow life, as nature did every spring. With the warmth came renewed strength and recovery for the girl and boy.

Waiting to be of use, the girl had spent her days watching the big man and the two quiet women break up the fields from the old chair outside her hut. Comfortable. Content. Her tender, healing skin soothed by clean, dry clothes and her exposed wrists and ankles warmed by a soft knitted blanket. The boy had been nearby, always. In his hut to the side of the girl's. Until he moved into hers. Then they had felt the heat of the earth growing from their shared bed, where they warmed each other. In the soft light of the moon they had made plans to leave the compound and move on together. Build a future. After they paid the Black Mage back in labour.

It had been a perfect little life. Impossible to imagine only a month before. Then things had changed.

The girl knelt in the sun-baked dirt. She smoothed a hand over the disturbed soil and enjoyed the warmth of it. The seeds she planted were left just deep enough to germinate. It would rain overnight. The air was heavy with it. A perfect time to plant.

A sharp twinge in her wrist made her pause. She stood, holding her arm against her chest, not wanting to look at it. The boy knelt in the field ahead of her. The other women and the man were spread across the churned earth carrying their own seeds to be sprinkled and covered.

The girl rolled her wrist forward and back, to both sides, feeling a disconcerting clicking inside. A cold sweat broke out over her body. No, it was just a twinge from the planting. From all the work after so long at rest. From work she had never known at home, on the island.

She dropped her hand, ignoring the familiar pain. Too familiar. She looked at the boy in the hot sun and the feeling of his scabbed skin under her fingers filled her mind. She had worried she felt it on many occasions since she first noticed it, when they came together in their joy at being alive.

The girl walked towards him. He knelt, his shoulder blades exposed in the thin shirt he wore. The scars were almost gone but she saw something else there. The roughness she had felt in the early spring wasn't truly a scab. Or not only a scab.

Of course it wasn't. Neither had the next one she felt been, or the next one. As the true scars healed the boy's skin had become light again. But the girl saw shadows growing under it that meant it wouldn't be long before something broke the surface. Something that didn't belong. She knew they must be in her skin as well, though the boy wouldn't admit to it. He said there was nothing in his either. He said she imagined it. That she saw something that wasn't there. He doubted her words. Her mind. He didn't listen to her anymore.

She tried to listen to him. Because she wanted to dream of the future. She wanted to live, and she wanted him to live too. He said they were cured. He said she was wrong. Wasn't that better than what she saw? It was becoming hard to delude herself though. She couldn't be quiet anymore, and the boy grew angry and annoyed at her ceaseless concern.

The boy wasn't actively planting. He knelt and stared at the soil without moving. She touched his shoulder, feeling compelled to run her fingers along his skin in search of the feathers inside it, about to break through. He flinched away from her touch before she could find more than the heat of him. He stood and looked down at her.

"Were you taking a break?" she asked.

"Just a short one." He turned away, moving on in the field and beginning to drop seeds and turn the soil over to cover them again. "I'm fine."

A cold response. It deserved the same in return but she worried about him.

"You don't look fine," she said too loudly as she chased him. The women and the man in the field looked up. The girl shrunk under their gazes. They were not unfriendly but they were still strangers, and they belonged to the Black Mage. What would they tell the young woman about the girl if they knew what she hid?

The girl moved in front of the boy, blocking him from continuing and drawing him to the side, facing away from the other planters.

"What's wrong? Do you feel it coming back?"

The annoyance returned to his eyes. She had quickly learned that he was good for hope. Good for action. Had been good when they needed the will to complete the impossible journey to the compound with nothing but some scraps and a bare idea of where they were going. He had even been good for a short while after they were 'cured'. Thinking only of her and of life. Loving her, loving life. So excited for the future they would have together.

But it had gone downhill from there. As they healed—in the bed they shared, as they waited to work—he had begun to obsess over their future. Over what it meant to have nothing. Two poor souls with no family and no home to go back to. Nothing to take with them when they left. He looked for ways to fix it and reacted badly to her worries that none of it would matter.

Her interest in his mood and wellbeing irked him. Her protectiveness only pushed him away.

"If you feel it—" she said, but he stepped towards her, his countenance threatening.

She backed up, tripping on an exposed root and nearly falling. She dropped the bag of seeds she'd been carrying and breathed a sigh of relief when they didn't spill.

"You're afraid of me," the boy said. Genuine regret showed in his eyes.

"I'm not afraid of you. I'm scared *for* you. If we're not cured then the Black Mage must operate again."

"I *am* cured."

She had tried the same before and it never worked.

"Am I?" she asked.

His eyes softened. He loved her. He did. And she loved him too. His gaze flitted to the other planters. One of the women rested and drank water. The big man and the other woman worked. In the distance, by the main building, a figure in black watched.

"We can talk when the work is done," he said.

He went back to dropping seeds and she shrunk down in the soil in his wake. She twisted her wrist again and felt the twinge. Something worked against its proper function, from deep inside. She pulled back her long sleeve, meant to protect her healing skin from the sun, and examined the visible bone. It was noticeably notched, but that could be from the surgery. Yet the surgery scars had healed.

She rolled it and watched how it moved. She listened and heard the click. Or did she hear it? Was it only in her mind? Had the bone always looked like that? At least when she had known she was changing, known the differences in her body meant she would die, she hadn't had anything to worry about. She had accepted it. Now she didn't know what she was. What she had to look forward to. Freedom and safety? A life? Or was it still death?

The girl stood and left her bag of seeds where it lay. She walked across the field in the direction of the huts and held herself to a reasonable pace. She wanted to run. She wanted to tear blindly across the earth she had helped to sow with seed minutes, hours before, and scuff it all up as she went. She wanted to rip her hair out.

She managed to cross the field without drawing attention. The Black Mage remained by the main building, her clothing long and dark and heavy though the sun was hot. The young woman didn't turn to follow the girl. She seemed to be watching the boy. Or looking into the middle distance at nothing.

The girl passed the main buildings and came to the huts, still walking. She balled her hands into fists so tight blood dripped from them as her nails dug into her palms. The pain of that alone kept her focus. Stopped her from doing more. Stopped her from screaming.

She pushed the door to their hut open more forcefully than normal but no one was watching now. Her clothes felt constricting and as she crossed the small space she tore at them. Enough to remove them but not seriously damage them, though the resistance made her want to destroy them. She made a small strangled sound she originally didn't know was her, though she felt the low hum in her chest. She felt her heart beat frantically in her ears.

There was a small mirror somewhere. She threw things around until she found it. Turned it to herself and looked. Examined. Obsessively pursued. Poured over what she could dimly see reflected back at her. Was her skin a normal tone? Was it shadowed? Was that, there, a dark feather deep below? A vein? One natural to humans or an aberration marking her a monster? She ran her bloodied hands over it and dug her nails into the blue line.

"What are you doing?"

The boy's outraged voice from the door. Then concern and movement and his solidity behind her.

"Stop!" He took her arms in his hands as her blood spurted across them both, dark and wet. Black and poisoned. "Why would you do this?"

She fought him. She wanted to fight him, not only for this. She wanted to fight him because he chose to remain ignorant. He refused to help himself.

She wanted to give in to his restraint because she wanted to be saved. Needed to be. But she also wanted to destroy herself. Because what was the point of living if feathers and bone spurs and deformations plagued her again? If the Black Mage had failed in healing them once, what was there to guarantee she could succeed if she tried again? What guarantee was there that the cure was even real?

The girl gave in to the boy's wiry strength. Her wrists hurt enough from his grip that she didn't need to do more. She relaxed against his chest.

He held her like that, too tight, for a few moments longer. The pain in her wrists grew great enough to hide the sharp pain of the gash across the base of her neck where she had broken the skin with her nails. Long nails. Human nails, or monstrous?

His breath was fast and hot by her ear.

"Was it a feather?" he whispered.

Tears grew at the edges of her eyes, blurring her vision. "I don't think so."

He loosened his grip on her wrists. "Let me look."

She lay against him, not wanting to turn. Not wanting to look into his eyes. Not wanting to acknowledge that she worried for him, yes, but she also worried for herself.

Eventually she turned and they faced each other. Blood dripped down her chest and was smeared where he had grabbed her. It obscured the injury.

"It doesn't look too bad," he said. "Lots of blood though. I'll get a cloth."

She sat on the edge of the bed and waited for him. The frenzied need to rid her body of whatever it was had left her. Now she felt like sleeping. She closed her eyes and breathed slowly. His gentle touch seemed to wake her from a sleep she didn't know she was in. He put a hand on her elbow and when she opened her eyes she found his face close to hers.

He cleaned the area around the cut with the damp cloth and a bowl of cold water that quickly ran dark with her blood. The girl looked away, not wanting to see what was revealed. She imagined what it would be. The rough edge of a feather poking through broken skin, black barbs caked with clotting blood. She shuddered. There would be bone spurs in her wrists. In her arms and elbows and the back of her neck. She remembered them, for they had been there, and they had been real. The Black Mage may have cut them out of her, excised them from deep within, but what guaranteed that they wouldn't come back?

"It's nothing," the boy said, bringing her back to the moment, seated before him and meeting his gaze. "Might have just been a vein. Which explains the blood."

She did cry then. Relief, hot and cold at once, poured through her. She leaned into him and pressed her body against him in the fight for life. Not an aberration. Just a human body. She had more time. She ran her fingers along his shoulder blades and stopped abruptly at the feel of roughness.

Did they really have more time? Sobs wracked her and the fall of her tears redoubled. Maybe it hadn't been a feather in *her* skin, but what she felt now was definitely one in his.

THE GIRL STOOD OUTSIDE the boy's hut in the mid-summer wind. It whipped her hair around her face and fluttered her clothes as she waited. He had left their hut for his own shortly after she found the first unmistakeable feather on his body—the first she could pull and force him to see—making him confront the reality of their future.

Now he refused to come out.

"Please," the girl said. "I want to see you."

No one had bothered them after the planting was done. The maintenance of the farm wasn't enough to require the two extra bodies to work. The girl helped in the main building on occasion—the Black Mage and her aids sold potions and strange plants to the people. Food and water were still provided to them. There was no other reason for the Black Mage or her people to involve themselves with the boy. Soon it would be time for the harvest and he would be wanted for that. If he would only come out.

The girl knocked again. There was no answer. She waited.

Her feathers and bone spurs were coming back too. What had taken years to form before had appeared in weeks. She shrugged the shawl she had wrapped around her higher to hide the telltale boniness at her neck, obscure the shadows under her skin that marked her as a monster. It came on slower than the boy's, but just as surely. The pain was coming back too. The girl wasn't sure she'd be able to help with the harvest when it was time. Unless she saw the Black Mage first.

"Is he in there?"

The Black Mage stood behind the girl, having approached seemingly without sound. She wore the hooded cloak as she always did, and the gloves. The big man was with her. The only man on the compound other than the boy.

The big man scared the girl now, but only because of his slow strength and what he could do with it if he was ever violent. Not that he had been. But she had never stopped looking at the people around them as a threat, especially not since the change started again. The big man's quietness was also unnerving. He never seemed to speak. Not even with distance from the Black Mage, as the two women did.

The girl nodded and the Black Mage indicated the big man should force the door. He did and disappeared inside the hut. There was the sound of a scuffle and something broke. Then the boy's raised voice. Then silence.

The boy walked out ahead of the big man. It was clear things had progressed since the last time the girl saw him. He wore a loose white shirt that clearly showed the patterns under his skin, and he hid one of his hands in a fold of the cloth.

The big man pushed him when he hesitated in the doorway. The girl flinched. The boy stumbled and the man followed and pulled the cloth away. The girl's eyes widened.

The boy's hand was fully inhuman now. Not only adorned with the sharp nails they had seen before they were brought to the Black Mage's compound, but a wholly monstrous hand with animal claws meant for ripping flesh. Long, flexible black feathers extended down the length of his arm, more extensive than the girl had ever seen. The Black Mage stared at it, expressionless.

"You should have come to me sooner. Now it will have to be amputated."

The Black Mage turned towards the main building and the boy followed without a word, the big man on his heels.

The girl ran after them. "Amputated? You're going to take his hand?"

"And most of his arm, from what I can see."

"You can't do that!" the girl shouted as they entered the first room in the Black Mage's workshop. The big man led the boy into the room where the surgery would be completed.

"I told you before, nothing monstrous can remain or the cure will be incomplete." The Black Mage turned back to the girl before following. "It's what you came to me to have done."

"And it didn't work." The girl grabbed the young woman's arm. "Was it even meant to work?"

The Black Mage shook the girl's hand off and entered the surgery room. The big man was in the process of tying the boy down on the table.

"I'm sorry," the boy said when he saw the girl. "I really thought it was over. I was so happy with you. Making plans. When I realised they meant nothing I couldn't handle it."

"They still meant something."

"Not without a cure."

"We can go away from here," the girl said. "Use what time we have left together. The surgery didn't work the first time and I almost died."

"But I saved you. You'd do the same for me."

The Black Mage looked on impassively, but the big man remained in the room, his silent strength an assurance. A threat.

"The surgery is too extensive," the girl said. "You healed with magic. You saved me with magic. You could only do those things because it didn't work. If it works you'll die—unable to heal—and if it works on me I can't save you."

She felt a hand on her arm and she cringed away. She didn't want to be removed from the room. She didn't want to leave the boy and she didn't want the procedure done to him again when she was wary of its purpose and effectiveness. She turned to find the Black Mage there, the young woman's ice eyes boring into the girl's.

The hand on her arm was covered in the black gloves the Mage always wore, had never been seen to remove since they arrived. The girl met the Black Mage's disconcerting eyes. She stepped back—away from the outstretched arm—and pulled off the woman's glove.

The girl's eyes widened. The boy gasped and writhed on the table under his restraints. The Black Mage's hand was revealed, and it was just as monstrous as the boy's.

"You're a monster too," the girl whispered. "But you're a real monster! Are you even a Black Mage? What have you done to us?"

The Black Mage stared at her in silence for a moment before gesturing to the big man.

"Tie her down too. I'll be back to work on them both."

The big man advanced on the girl. She tried to run around him to the door but he caught her by the arm as she passed. He wrenched her shoulder back, lifted her bodily and slammed her down on the table next to the boy. The girl screamed but could do nothing to resist the man's iron strength and his great weight that pressed her down. The boy strained against his bonds but could not escape them.

The man left the room and they were alone together, all the fight gone from them.

"She's going to kill us," the girl said. "She's going to come back and kill us."

The boy was silent. Unmoving. The girl looked over at him and the visible sadness in him broke her heart. She knew he felt responsible for bringing them here, to this cure that was not a cure.

"We have to escape," she said. He turned his head to her. "We can't give up now."

He pushed listlessly against the bonds. "The restraints are too strong. I can't get out so there's no way you can."

"There must be magic we can use. There always has been before. Hurry, think, before she comes back."

The boy furrowed his brow as if considering, but then he closed his eyes and his body went limp. "I'm sorry I hid from you. I'm sorry I wanted to pretend."

"Don't apologise. We're going to get out."

The girl looked down at what she could see of her body. She couldn't access anything with her hands, tied at her sides as they were. She couldn't reach the boy. So what could she do? The boy turned towards her, his dark eyes mournful.

"What magic is there?" she asked.

"I bet you wish you were the one to read those books."

"Of course I do. I still don't really believe you can read."

He laughed, his smile—not seen for a long time—lighting up her heart for a fleeting moment. His teeth were long and sharp now, his jaw seeming to have changed as well. The girl ran her tongue over her own teeth. Had her face changed shape? She didn't look at herself anymore.

"What could you do with blood?" she asked. "When you bit me, what happened?"

"I can't reach you now," he said.

"But what happened?"

"Similar to the other times. Rage. Frenzied strength. Life."

"That didn't happen to me."

He didn't answer. She felt her teeth again. Then before she could change her mind she bit through her tongue.

The pain was paralysing. It flowed over her like serrated lightning. Violent and all-encompassing.

Nothing happened. She bit again, raking what was left of her tongue back through the razor sharp teeth she now found natural in her mouth. Monstrous teeth that did not belong on a human person. She still wasn't sure if anything had happened until she tried to look at the boy.

He moved slowly, his eyes large and bright. He looked strange, otherworldly, and that's when she knew it was working. She pushed against the bonds, remembering how the boy had cracked that man's neck with his bare hands, and thinking back, how her blood had let her hold on to a disintegrating raft in a storm fit to shatter ships. Her mind had seemed more affected, but her body must have been too. She clenched her fists, the newly sharp nails digging into her palms. She shouted and broke the straps.

The girl stood. She wanted to leave the room and break the Black Mage's neck like the boy had done to the bad man with the wagon. But she had to free the boy first. She stumbled to the other side of the operating table and cut the straps holding his arms with her claws. They really were claws now, rather than nails.

As she left the boy to free himself she felt compelled to check the storage on the walls of the room. She threw open the cabinets to find dried bones and gory feathers and misshapen skulls and what looked like strips of dried flesh. The girl took a step back at the sight. What pieces here were theirs? What more would the Black Mage have taken from them if they hadn't escaped? The girl took another step away in horror before realising what she needed to do.

"The flint," she said clearly, though a minute ago she couldn't have articulated anything. Her tongue was whole already.

The boy rose behind her and searched in his pants pocket. The big man hadn't had time to remove his clothes. The boy offered the life-saving tools to her when he found them.

"We'll go out the window." The girl struck the flint on steel even though there was nothing for it to catch on. A tiny spark bloomed and floated on the air. It moved slowly in front of her eyes. *Burn*. The girl felt the fire that would grow from that spark. The fire that didn't exist yet but would. She fed it. Moved it to the cabinets that held the leftover parts of those who had been there before the girl and the boy. The parts that might even belong to them. "But first, we'll burn it all."

The feathers ignited, burning up in bright swirls of red and orange. Then the wood beneath them caught and time sped up. The flames rose to engulf the entire wall of the room. The girl backed away towards the boy and watched with horrified fascination how quickly the fire spread. The door to the main room opened and black smoke was pulled through as the air exchanged.

The boy's mind grew loud beside the girl's as she breathed the dark soot of the fire. She felt his pain from the transformation but it was nothing like the pain he had been in when they first arrived. He was alert and strong and very alive. That was good. Then suddenly the girl felt the Black Mage's mind as well.

The young woman was surprised, able to feel the girl and boy too. She must never have done this with any of the others. The girl showed the Black Mage what could be done with the fire. She reached out to the dead in the smoke. She moved through the bones in the earth to every fire in the compound. She felt the fire under the earth that led to the fire back on the island, beneath the mountain. Death in the earth. Death in its lifeblood.

The Black Mage recoiled from the power the girl could command. Her mind didn't join in it but shrunk from it. She cowered in the other room and was afraid.

The girl took the boy's hand and led him to the window. It was barred like everything else in the operating room but the boy broke through easily and ducked under the remaining glass shards, heedless of the cuts they left in his arms and back. The girl followed. The stinging pain the broken glass wrought in her felt like power. The blood dripping off her felt like life.

She left the burning building behind and followed the boy into the field. The Black Mage's horrified thoughts faded as they ran.

THE GIRL LOOKED BACK at the burning compound from where she stood in the field. The uncanny fire had spread to the other buildings and its red light lit up the darkening sky. The scene reminded the girl of their escape from the village. How the boy had burned their home to save her.

She looked down at him, lying in the grass. He slept fitfully. Too exhausted after the events in the operating room to go on but not yet safe enough to fully succumb. Now she was the one who had saved him with fire.

But this time was different. She had no hope of a cure to offer him when he woke. They escaped to nothing. Only more pain and eventual death.

She wished he would get up, so they could continue to run in case the Black Mage or any of her aids survived the fire. Best to put some distance between them and the compound before the big man came for them. But the girl was tired too, and sore, and stiff from the transformation. She knelt by the boy and put a hand on his shoulder. He murmured at her touch and his sleep became less fitful, but he did not wake.

The girl looked up to find a shadow against the night's fire. A dark silhouette.

"In all the time I've done this," the Black Mage said into the stillness, "I've never seen power like yours. Though I've never actually seen smoke used to trigger the magic. I knew it could be done, but it's too wild for what I do, too likely to doom me."

The girl relaxed. The Black Mage's tone wasn't threatening despite that her home had been destroyed.

"How long have you done this?" the girl asked.

"Six years."

The Black Mage moved to sit wearily on the grass. The girl had never seen her show any sign of weakness. It appeared that with the fire had gone the icy calm surrounding the young woman. Her gloves were also gone, and her hood pulled back to reveal shining black hair and protruding bones at her collar. Now that the girl had time to really look at them, she thought the Black Mage's hands might be in a state between the girl's hands and the boy's. They were clawed, and small feathers ran along the backs of them, but they were still mostly human.

"You've lived with this for six years?" the girl asked.

"Six years since I left my village, almost ten since I knew what I was."

"I never thought we'd have that long."

"You won't." The Black Mage stared back at the burning compound with blankness in her eyes. "You'll be dead within a year." She indicated the sleeping boy. "He has less than half that."

"Or we'll be monsters," the girl said without thinking.

"Maybe. Have you heard stories of monsters in this world? Living beyond the villages?"

The girl shook her head. It was a fair point. If any of the emerging monsters had survived there would be monsters in the world. "Maybe they're not monstrous though."

The Black Mage smiled sadly. She didn't respond and the girl appreciated her reserve in not immediately disagreeing. But the girl also wasn't sure she was wrong. The boy had been presented with the chance to be a monster in truth, even the girl had been given that chance many times since they left the island. Every time they had rejected it.

"How did you last these six years?" the girl asked.

"The cure."

The girl turned to the Black Mage, the spreading warmth of hope growing in her chest. "So it does exist?"

The Black Mage laughed mirthlessly. "No. There is no cure. But the story of it draws those who survive their loved ones to me, and I use them." She met the girl's eyes with her unnaturally cold gaze. "You should join me. You can even keep him if you want. I can keep you alive longer with magic. Manage your pain with the surgeries if you need."

"You remove your own growths?"

"I don't, anymore. It helps with the pain but it only speeds up the transformation. Any magic performed with my own blood or body parts does too. Magic performed with the parts of others doesn't seem to. That has saved me all these years. I've tried everything and magic can't stop it. But it *can* slow it."

"That's why you do this."

"I refuse to give up." The Black Mage shrugged in the night. "I can't just fade away."

"So there truly is no cure." The girl sat back with the knowledge. The boy breathed softly beside her, her hand on his back. He had been so sure. His hope had brought them to the compound and kept them alive this long. "What about the two women and the man? The one woman indicated you had cured her, and we assumed the same was true of the others."

"Didn't you notice that their scars don't heal? Yours faded shortly after your first surgery, but theirs do not."

The girl frowned. "They were never monsters."

"Only people with no one to love them. With nowhere to go. Some fleeing family or friends who hurt them. The man came from my village. Followed me into the night when I left. A little magic and he was mine. Same with the women, only later. They believe the stories they told you. I believe they're happy with their lot. They'll help me rebuild."

The girl sat in silence for a while, watching the fire. The boy slept on, oblivious to their conversation.

"Maybe you shouldn't rebuild," the girl said. "Stop this and come with us instead."

The Black Mage shook her head. "Where will you go? What will you do?"

"I don't know yet. But not this."

The Black Mage looked down at the sleeping boy.

"There was a boy in my village too. His death..." She took a deep breath. "His gruesome, horrifying death, enacted on him in front of me, in front of everyone in the village, spurred me to leave. I've never gotten two of you at once before. Those who come to me have all come alone."

"You don't have to be alone," the girl said.

"I'm not. Not really. I have my people."

The girl didn't mention that the people never spoke. That they were little more than voiceless thralls.

"I was thrown off when you arrived together," the Black Mage continued. "That's why I was going to let you die."

Now the girl understood why she had barely survived the surgery when the boy had done so easily. She hadn't been meant to survive.

"He was clearly stronger, and delivered a much higher yield. Much less likely to work against me without you. Were you in love before you left? Is that how you both came to be here?"

"No." The girl blushed but knew the dark night hid it. "We didn't really know each other. But he saved me. I was discovered. I would have died in our village just like the boy in yours, and he would have come to you alone. But he didn't watch me die. He fought them. He chose to make things harder on himself and take me with him when he left."

"Would you have saved him?"

The girl considered the question. There was no reason to lie. She was back to the place she had been before. No reason to lie because there was nowhere to go from here. This was it. All there was.

"No," she said. "I wouldn't have thought I could."

The Black Mage's tense body relaxed.

"And I wouldn't have thought it would change anything," the girl continued, turning to the Black Mage. "I wouldn't have thought there was a point. He saved me because he thought there was a cure." The girl looked up at the burning buildings, finally giving voice to something she had learned. "But we still have a future even without a cure. As long as we're alive we have a future."

The Black Mage looked at the ground. "The idea of a cure is old lore. Something invented to give hope, I assume. Something used by the real Black Mages to lure the monsters to them. That's what was done to me. It's how I came to be in this place. And it's what I have done with it since."

The girl noticed the sound of the boy's sleeping breath had ceased just as he wrapped his hands around the Black Mage's throat from behind.

"Why should I let you live after what you've done to us?" he whispered. "To the others?"

So he had been listening. The girl almost moved to stop him but what he said was true. The Black Mage would continue to kill people if they let her go free.

"You should join me," the Black Mage said calmly, though her voice was strained as the boy pressed on her jugular. "Join me and you can live."

"Not like this I won't," the boy said. "You're a real monster."

Now the girl did intervene. "There's no cure."

The boy turned to her. His eyes were wide in the moonlight and the red reflected on the sky from the still-burning fire.

"Remember how good we felt after the first surgery?" the girl asked. "Did you ever think you'd feel like that again? If she relieves their pain, gives them hope, and more time..."

"You'd forgive what she's done?"

"She's just trying to live. She fed us, clothed us, gave us a place to stay and a reason to go on. She was never unkind to us."

The girl stood and motioned for the boy to join her. Reluctantly he let go of the young woman and stood. He took the girl's hand with his affected one, the sharpness of the jutting bone and the spurs on it rigid against her still-soft, mostly human hand.

"You should join *us* instead," the girl said.

The Black Mage remained seated, not looking up at them, the fire that burned everything she had built reflected in her eyes. "And die?"

"And live, for now." The girl shared a look with the boy, the feel of his mind flaring against hers as the magic was still present in her blood. "I have room to love you too, for as long as we have left."

The woman still didn't look at them. "I can't."

The girl went to speak again but the boy pulled her away. She pushed him off and turned back. "Why not?"

"I'd kill you." The Black Mage stood and looked her in the eyes. "For your blood and bones. I'd kill you both if it meant I could live longer. I told you I don't want to fade away."

The boy took the girl's hand and led her towards the tree-line they had emerged from a season ago. The girl looked back to see the Black Mage's silhouette against the flames. As she watched, the Black Mage pulled her hood up over her hair and strode away.

THE GIRL DUCKED UNDER the rock overhang and moved slowly into the recess in the mountain. Her eyesight was much better than it had been before the transformation sped up but it was still worse than the boy's. He was deep inside this time. She could barely see when she got to the place he rested.

He lay in a slight depression in the cave floor, breathing noisily. The girl listened to see if he spoke nonsense under his breath—the pain had rendered him delirious more than once—but he slept instead. It seemed to be less terrible for him now. The girl was finally getting used to the pain, as it invaded every part of her, as it became more natural than comfort. It must be the same for him. He had been bad for a while and then things had gotten slightly better. Now he slept most of the time to avoid it all.

The girl remembered once again what the Black Mage had said about using the magic from the body parts of others to slow it. They might have harvested each other in an attempt to prolong their lives together. But the girl hadn't been willing to use the boy and he had recoiled at the idea of harming her. There was no cure. They had decided it was best to transform together, naturally.

As the girl drew closer the boy tensed in his sleep, monstrous senses detecting her even while at rest. He flowed up as she reached out to touch him.

"It's just me," she said when he grabbed her, his monstrous claws coming to encircle her arms, pressing down the feathers. He backed off as quickly as he had attacked. He used to feel guilty for his animal actions and apologised frequently, but now he didn't say a word. She settled down beside him.

"I thought you weren't coming back this time." He rolled over to look at her. She couldn't see the details of his face but as he shifted the low light reflected off his transforming eyes. Two iridescent points in the darkness. "You should really go and not come back."

"What would be the point of that? Where else could I find another monster like me?"

He laughed softly. She moved closer. His transformation continued to progress more quickly than hers. He still hid from her, far back in the shadows under the earth, where she couldn't see the extent of the changes. But he didn't really know how bad hers were either, at least not physically, unless his eyesight was better than she thought.

It had also started to affect her mind, and she kept that secret fiercely. More than once when she left the cave for food she had found herself far from the boy, not sure how she'd gotten there. One time she had come back to herself while standing on the edge of a cliff that looked out to the sea, not far from the cave through the forest. She had seen their old island and the great mountain that held fire, let her bare, clawed foot slide over the precipice, wondering what would happen if she fell.

Another time she found herself standing over the corpse of a deer, covered in blood, all over her hands, arms, and face. Must have found it dead and started eating. Or maybe she had killed it herself. She hadn't been sure.

So far she had always recovered her senses enough to come back. She had to. The boy needed her.

They didn't struggle for food or water at least—their monstrous guts able to digest flesh and blood and bones raw and tolerate water straight from the streams or ponds—and the cave had been as comfortable a sleeping place as any would be now that their bodies hurt so. If they weren't dying it wouldn't be such a bad life.

They were far from the Black Mage's meadow and far from the place the girl thought the muddy little road passed through the forest. If no one found them they should be able to wait out the transformation in their cave. To die together.

"I won't leave you," the girl said. "We started this journey together and we'll finish it together."

He might have smiled. It was hard to tell.

"I'm sorry—" he started to say. The same old apology. That the cure wasn't real. That he had given her hope when she never should have had any. That he had saved her in the first place, keeping her alive only to suffer through this.

"I always knew I was going to die," she said, cutting him off before he could make them both upset. "But I thought it would be brutal and at the hands of my family and friends. And I thought I'd be alone."

His bright eyes remained open, focused on her, the only thing she could reliably see.

"Now I have you." She struggled to keep emotion out of her voice. "Just hold on a little longer. Hold on to what you were. What you are. Stay with me until it's time for both of us to go."

"I can't," he whispered. "I can't do it anymore."

"Please. Hold on to your heart. To mine. It won't be long for me either."

She lay down beside him and he held her. They had long ceased to be able to do any more to comfort each other. The large protrusions of bone at his joints dug into her, and her own must be doing the same to him, but she didn't complain and neither did he. The feathers, at least, were soft. His heart beat steadily against her back. She listened to it with her body. Still the same. When his breathing had returned to the slightly more peaceful rhythm of sleep, she slipped out of his grasp and carefully made her way into the light.

She reached into the sun with a monstrous hand and arm she never would have recognised as her own if she hadn't seen the transformation take place herself. Long feathers covered her, and sharp bones protruded all over, her very structure changed. She refused to look at her reflection in the water to see the extent of it, but she didn't think anyone would know her as human. The boy was likely worse. She had felt the massive bones and sinew and feathers that grew from him in the dark. They were a part of him now and she loved them just the same.

The girl looked through the trees that masked their hiding spot to see if there was anyone around. She kept a watch for signs of other people just in case they had to move. So far there had been none. The great forest was quiet near the shore. There was no reason for anyone to be out there.

She turned back. She never stood in the light for long. Just enough time to feel the sun. To feel alive. To feel like a person worthy of being seen by the world, even though she was actually a monster, and being seen was the worst thing she could do.

She returned to the cave to sit in darkness. The day didn't feel like it belonged to her anymore. She looked at the sleeping boy—or sleeping monster, whatever he was now—and felt tears slide down her cheeks. She must still be human if she could cry.

THE GIRL LUMBERED INTO the cave, breathing heavily. The muffled rhythm of a lone drum followed her.

"Wake up," she said. "We have to leave."

The boy groaned in the dark, his changed form more visible to her changed eyes than it had been the last time she'd seen him. She took him in, not wanting to pretend he was something else now, at the end. It was easier to look at him than it was to look at herself, though she knew she had changed as much. The pain had become a part of her, easy to live with. Seeing that on him was harder. She ran her clawed hands over his feathered skin, black against the blackness.

"I can't leave the cave," he said.

"They're coming for us. I don't know if they'll be able to find the cave, but they're out there and they're coming. We have to move."

Feathers and limbs shifted in the shadows. One of his monstrous eyes opened and looked back at her. He didn't get up. This had become her greatest worry. That he might not get up and run when the time came.

"I don't want to anymore."

"Please," she said. "At least try with me. Remember when you dragged me through the snow on the island? I came with you, for all of this. Please."

"You came with me for a cure. There is no hope now."

She shook her head. "I didn't know about the cure then, remember? I still followed you."

The second monstrous eye opened, and he moved. Slowly. Laboriously. They wouldn't get far in the state they were in. But they had to try. Just one last time.

They hadn't used the magic since they left the Black Mage's compound. They hadn't wanted to accelerate their transformations and neither of them knew how to use it to remove their pain or slow it. The magic had no use for them once they had chosen not to fight.

But now...

"One more time?" she asked the boy.

"One last time."

The girl fumbled in the half-light, disturbing things that had been stowed in reverence upon their arrival but left to gather dust since. The mortar and pestle. The flint and steel. She picked up the last two and struck them together. A quickly dying spark sputtered for a moment before extinguishing.

She took a handful of dry leaves from the pile beside the old fire pit. They never started fires anymore. The cold barely affected them and the light bothered the boy. But the girl had left the leaves there for this very purpose, just in case.

She struck the flint again and the spark that came off it nestled into the leaves and grew. The boy moved behind her, coming to rest over the fire. White smoke curled towards them in the faltering light. The girl took a feather from the nape of her neck and added it to the fitful flame. Then she took a whole handful from her chest, tiny pinpricks in her mostly senseless skin. The smoke grew black and thick, the fire almost suffocating under the weight of her additions.

The girl put a hand on the boy's chest, feeling the difficulty he had breathing in the thick smoke. They coughed. They breathed deeply and coughed again. The boy put his hand on her chest as well. They breathed.

Their minds came together and their hearts beat at the same rate. A moment of peace in the faded pain, in the nearly complete change. But the drum grew louder and others joined it. The fire burned. The girl looked into the boy's eyes and her mind told him it was time to leave.

They walked out into snow. It had been the first snowfall the girl saw since last year when everything in her life was outwardly normal. When people had looked at her like she was a young girl, beautiful and full of potential. Before they'd seen a monster and the expressions on their faces had changed to hatred and fear.

The snow was blindingly white after the cave and the girl stood stunned for a moment. The drums were much louder outside. Close. Maybe the person who spotted the girl, black against the white, had followed her back. How else could they know where the monsters rested?

When the girl's eyes adjusted, she ran to the trees that shielded the cave and saw the people far away and downhill, trudging through the snow. To come for them. To kill them, finally.

But even though she had known death was inevitable for so long, she found she didn't want to be killed. Dying was one thing, but to be killed by people who didn't know her, who had no reason to seek her out, when she had done nothing wrong. When she rested and waited to die in silence, harming no one. That was different.

The girl ran back to the boy, her vision sliding and distorting the world. The death in the ground and the death the drums meant to bring sang in her blood. The boy's dying mind floated there with it.

She took his monstrous hand and led him away. They ran through the trees and ran from the drums. A shout rang out below as they ran along a ledge, black feathered bodies stark against the snow. The people had seen them. People from the village near the Black Mage's compound, no doubt. It was too bad the girl and the boy hadn't travelled farther to find their final resting place, but they had been too weak and in too much pain. They had gone as far as they could and settled, and it hadn't made sense to move again.

The girl had no plan. She ran and the boy ran with her. But as they ran she came to realise she was headed for the cliff. Headed to the spot they could stare out over the sea and look back to their old home, the island. She stopped, prompting the boy to stop too. Why go there, if not to die? What could they do on a cliff looking out over the water? The people would follow them, and they would have nowhere left to go except to their deaths.

But there was nowhere else to go already. The girl started again and the boy followed. There was a time he had run to the edge of a black sand beach, no boat to be had, and she had followed him then. That initial run hadn't seemed to have a destination other than death, and look where it had taken them. The boy had given her that. Now she was the one who meant to give him hope. If not hope to live, at least hope not to be butchered by strangers, despairing in a dark cave.

They ran up the slope towards the cliff's edge. The girl's breathing was hard now and the boy puffed behind her. The smoke from the fire had given them the strength they needed to move. To run. To try. False hope, but something. The opening of the trees into the sky above shone like salvation.

The drums beat loudly. Angry shouts echoed in the girl's ears. She broke through the trees and stood in the open air, the light revealing her for all to see. She stopped at the edge of the cliff and looked back. The boy stepped up to stand with her.

Stillness.

The power in the girl's blood rang out. Her heart thudded from the exertion and it matched the pulse beneath the earth. She saw the island and its fire-mountain, distant, like their lives before the change. The death it held in its bowels was nearer, linked to the fires beneath the mainland, linked to the core of the earth.

The fire was death. Made of it and made for it. Old as everything. Not yet awake and aware of its potential. The boy looked into her eyes and she knew he felt it too. Just like they had felt the heat in the mountain on the night they escaped.

She could burn the whole world if she wanted to. She could destroy all the people who chased those they perceived to be monsters but knew nothing about. Who would kill them just as surely as they breathed. Life was nothing but death waiting to happen. The girl knew that better than anyone.

The boy's eyes were bright and monstrous but behind them the girl still saw the human he used to be. His heart was still human and so was hers. He gave her the choice of what to do. He felt the opportunity as surely as she did and he left it to her, as he had left it to her to decide what they would do with the Black Mage.

She let the fire go. Though they were chased by monsters, they themselves were not monsters. Not even at the end.

The girl looked back at the people charging up the mountain. Coming with torches and drums and evil knives and hammers and scythes. She saw the faces of her family members the night they'd tried to kill her. She saw the faces of the man and young woman whose distraction had saved the girl and boy an early death on a wagon, joining the mob, returning to end what they had inadvertently allowed to go on. She saw them all. And turned away.

Free air hung above the sea. The girl opened her mouth to speak and found she no longer had a voice. But she knew she didn't need one.

Come with me, her mind said.

I will, the boy's answered without hesitation.

The drums beat their footsteps—their heartbeats—as they ran to the cliff's edge and didn't stop. The girl pushed off the rim of the world and felt the boy come with her. The wind whistled past changed limbs and changed torsos and black feathers as they fell into the blue sky, the blue of the sea coming up to meet them.

There was no pain in the sky—the girl's body finally free of the pressure of the earth. She closed her eyes. And opened her wings.

THE END

Afterword

YOUR BLOOD AND BONES was written by a song.

In December 2020, I was newly pregnant with my third child, but I didn't know yet. It was in that altered state that I woke in the middle of the night with an irresistible urge to listen to "King and Lionheart" by the band, Of Monsters and Men. The urge was so strong that I picked up my phone, googled the song, and was about to play it before I realised: it's 2AM and my husband is sleeping beside me. This is not a good idea! Especially since I don't own or use headphones. I managed not to play it, but as soon as I woke in the morning the urge returned.

I played "King and Lionheart" on repeat a few times before I forgot to stop our google music from moving on. It cycled through a couple familiar Of Monsters and Men songs until it got to "Your Bones", which was new to me. I liked it enough that my "King and Lionheart" obsession was cured, and instead I played "Your Bones" on repeat for the next two weeks. As I listened to it, YOUR BLOOD AND BONES grew in my mind, until I knew the entire story.

If the constant repetition wasn't bad enough for the others in our household, I also spent this time shouting nonsensical things out loud like "YES, that's what happens next! Exactly!" Suffice to say early pregnancy doesn't agree with me... or does it? :D. I love this little book, and I'm not sure I'd have come up with it in any other state.

I told the story that emerged (from ~two hundred replays of "Your Bones") to my husband on Christmas Eve while we were up late putting together a last minute Christmas present (a big bed for our three year old!). He was a little surprised by it but thought it was interesting enough to listen to again when I wrote it and read it aloud to him a few months later.

Maybe one day someone from Of Monsters and Men will read YOUR BLOOD AND BONES and recognise their song in it.

Acknowledgements

Thank you to my husband, Ragnar, for giving me the time away from our kids that I needed to write this novella. Thank you for sitting with me while I described this strange story late into the night on Christmas Eve in 2020, and for listening to me read the whole thing out loud once it was written.

Thank you to my brother, critique partner, and first reader, Mike, for your comments and edits.

Thank you to the band, Of Monsters and Men, for the song that inspired this story.

Thank you to my cover artist, Jenna Vincent, for so beautifully representing YOUR BLOOD AND BONES in art.

Thank you to Virginia McClain, for the lovely design for all formats of the cover.

And thank you to the unknown writer on a forgotten panel at the online Nebulas in 2020, for saying that "a novella is about *one* thing". I understood you, and then I wrote YOUR BLOOD AND BONES.

Also by J. Patricia Anderson

DAUGHTERS OF TITH

The kandar are the children of the trees. Powerful. Immutable. Nine hundred eternal beings who need no sleep nor sustenance, created at the beginning of time to guard the nine human Earths.

That was never meant to change.

The youngest of five sisters, Tchardin is about to be acknowledged as queen of the kandar. She must lead them in their Creator-given Purpose–to guide and inspire the humans–but her people have been exiled to their homeworld for generations. None of them have seen the Earths. Not one of them has met a human.

Tchardin can think of no way to end their exile until a strange longing calls her from beyond the shore of their island. Most of her sisters tell her to ignore it, to take her place as queen and focus on the kandar. One suggests she answer it, as it might be the key to finally returning her people to their Purpose.

A different epic fantasy set on a non-Earth-like secondary world.

For fans of Guy Gavriel Kay, N. K. Jemisin, and Ann Leckie.

Printed in Great Britain
by Amazon